Anna

Stephen O'Sullivan

WP

Whimsical Publications, LLC

Florida

To purchase the authorized electronic edition of *Anna*, visit
www.whimsicalpublications.com

Cover art by Traci Markou
Editing by Melissa Hosack
Image for cover art © Alexandra Thompson

Published in the United States by
Whimsical Publications, LLC
Florida

ISBN-13: 978-1-940707-66-2

Printed in the United States of America

I continued to walk without any idea of where I was or where I was going. I wandered around stores to get in out of the cold more than to actually view the goods on sale. An eager sales clerk practically accosted me in a furniture store. I was looking at a settee and could not resist the temptation to sit down. The extravagant comfort was pure luxury as I sank deep into the soft cushions. He tried everything possible to talk me into purchasing it. In an effort to rid myself of him, I said the colour was not ideal and would clash with other furnishings. Poppycock, of course—the make-believe furnishings only existed in my make-believe house.

"No problem, miss," he said. "We can have the settee covered in any colour fabric that suits you."

Having failed with the colour clash idea, I tried another approach. "It might be too large for our sitting room," I said in my best la-de-da accent.

"You're in luck, miss. We also do have the same settee in a two-seater version," he said enthusiastically.

He was pushing enthusiasm over that fine line that divides eagerness and annoying persistence, but I still did not have the heart to tell him I wasn't interested. After all, if I couldn't afford a cup of tea, I could hardly afford an Italian designed settee.

"I do like it," I said. "But I'll have to bring my father in to see it first."

Eureka, it worked, although I was left feeling as if I had burst a child's balloon. His face lost all friendliness as he backed away. I guess he had heard the line or similar words to the same effect many times before.

It was early evening when I retraced my steps back down Dorset Street. Most of the small shops that lined both sides of the road had closed. I passed darkened windows and graffiti-covered shutters as late autumn leaves fluttered past, blown by a sharp, cold breeze.

Seventy-six Ignatius Road stood nestled between two similar terraced houses, and as I approached the door, I lacked the warm feeling of relief normally experienced when returning home on a cold, dark evening. I knocked on the door.

"Anna," Grandma said, welcoming me with a warm smile. "Come in, child, I've been waiting for you to come home."

She was alone in the house and brought me into the kitchen where the heat of the stove warmed the whole room. A white linen tablecloth covered the kitchen table, its edges finely decorated with an intricate lace pattern. A place was set and Grandma fussed over me as if I were a guest of honour.

"Is Peter not home?" I asked.

"No, he's gone out."

"And Grandpa?" I said.

"He's at the Workers' Club. He goes most nights."

"What's a Workers' Club?" I asked.

Her eyes turned upward. "Just another name for a public house. He thinks because it's a club restricted to *members* only, it can't be classed as boozing. He condemns Peter for going to the pub too often, yet he goes to his workers' club all the time. There's hypocrisy for you, don't you think?"

I smiled but remained silent. I wanted to agree and back up her condemnations of Grandpa with comments such as *the pot calling the kettle black*. I mean, she practically invited me to say something negative. But I said nothing, letting my smile answer the question.

I went to bed, as I had an early start in the morning. Twice I was awakened from my sleep. The first time was when Grandpa came home. I heard the front door being pulled shut and the noise of his heavy footsteps on the wooden stairs. The second time was when Peter came home. Even before I glanced at the clock, I knew it was an ungodly hour. His footsteps on the stairs were confused. It was as if his feet dragged and he took two steps back for every one forward. The silence of the night seemed to exaggerate every noise he made. I could hear him stumbling around his room for quite a while before he decided to go to bed. His bedsprings creaked in protest when he fell onto the mattress. Then there was a sudden silence and the quietness of the early hour once more asserted itself.

I closed my eyes and drifted back to sleep. But it was not a contented sleep, for I dreamt sad dreams peppered with visions of my mother. She was calling to me, warning me of what I did not know, for her words were distant and indefinable.

Acknowledgements

For my daughter, Freya.

One

Never before had I seen so many people in one place at the same time. I stood on the platform, suitcase in hand, and looking every bit the orphan as hordes of people hurried past. The rushing crowd bunched together and surged like a fast-flowing river through the ticket gate. I followed them and, despite trying to stay at the back of the mass, I found myself sucked into the human stream and swept along like a small fish that had inadvertently swam into a strong current. My arm ached as I hung on to my heavy suitcase, which was continuously thumped and bashed sideways as other cases collided with it and kneecaps nudged it from behind.

When I reached the gate, the people on either side of me passed through as if in a great momentous hurry. They, like those that had gone before them, held their tickets aloft and waved them at the railroad employee who stood checking them.

He was young, and his boyish appearance was exaggerated by an ill-fitting uniform that was several sizes too big for him. Even allowing for his oversized clothes, I guessed he was no more than a year or maybe two older than I was. I watched him through gaps in the lurching heads and shoulders before me. Although his head turned from side to side, he seemed uninterested in the tickets, simply going through the motions to give the impression he was doing his job. Or perhaps he was overwhelmed by the crowd and resigned himself to fact that his task was impossible? Well, maybe not impossible—he could have closed one side of the gate and let the arriving passengers through one by one, thus giving him time to check each ticket in turn. But the queue would have been intolerable, and I wondered without much seriousness if the mass of people would have rebelled and stormed the gate like an army of barbarians scaling the walls of an ancient fortified castle.

I, like the others, held up my ticket as I passed. I was unable to slow for fear I would be trampled by the unstoppable throngs of people from behind. I turned the ticket toward him so it would be easy for him to read. His eyes seemed lifeless as they blankly scanned it. He maintained the same vacant expression as I was swept by, and I suspected I could have waved any old scrap of paper and would have still been granted access through the black rusting gates.

Heuston Station was a dim and uninviting place, and despite the crowds, it reeked of loneliness. I felt the draughts on my bare legs and while, strangely enough I did not shiver, the chill crept into my bones where it seemed to radiate out until my entire body ached from the cold. The heaving crowd had dispersed in the large open area of the station and almost all had made straight for one of the various exit doors before disappearing out into the darkness. I looked around, but could see no sign of my uncle Peter, who was supposed to collect and bring me to my grandparents' house. I had never met my uncle and had no idea what he looked like, but it was obvious he was not there. The station had almost emptied of people and, from the few that remained, none matched the description of an anxious uncle looking for a lost niece.

A drunken man stumbled around at one of the entrance doors. His clothes were torn and threadbare. His furry hat had flaps that hung down over his ears but did little to cover his wild, matted hair. He had a bushy grey beard and the visible skin of his face appeared blackened, as if smudged with soot.

A man in a railroad uniform stood blocking him from entering. He held his arms out and was trying to shoo him away from the door. They seemed to be dancing a ridiculous dance that was without rhythm as the tramp tried to enter and the man in uniform strove to block his path. The official was taking great care not to touch the vagabond, as if fearful his dirty clothes would pass on some fatal disease. Absorbed by the silent antics of the two, I put down my case and sat upon it.

After a few minutes, the drunken man staggered away, furiously waving his arms and shouting a stream of obscenities. His torrent of foul language did not seem to be solely directed at the man that had blocked his path, but for anybody that might be within earshot of his slurred ranting.

I shivered, feeling desperately alone and unwanted. I stared at the entrance doors and into the dark street beyond, and wondered if anyone was coming for me or if I had been forgotten about.

"Anna?" The voice behind me was loud and I could not tell if the calling of my name was a question or an exclamation of surprise.

I stood and turned to see Uncle Peter facing me. While I had never met him, I knew beyond all doubt he was a relative. Perhaps it was his face that bore a vague resemblance to his sister, my mother.

"Uncle Peter?"

"Oh, Jesus, drop the uncle, will you? I'm not much older than yourself!"

He was right. Calling him uncle did seem silly, as he was only twenty-six and just nine years older than me. But he looked older. While Peter was tall and muscular, his face had a haggard look about it. He was not fat, but his face appeared bloated when compared to the rest of his body. And his cheeks, they were a sort of blotchy red with small veins visible here and there. I had seen that face many times before, but normally on men much older than Peter's twenty-six years. It was the face of a heavy drinker.

He stepped forward to hug me, and I felt as if I was being crushed to death by a bear. The stench of stale beer made me feel ill and it was a great relief when the bear finally released me. I stood back and tried to massage one of my crushed arms in such an inconspicuous way that it would not give offence.

"How was the journey?" he asked.

"Long, and the carriage was packed. Some people had to stand for the whole trip."

"That's because it's Sunday night," he said.

"Sunday?" I looked at him with confusion, wondering what Sunday had to do with it.

"Yeah, most of the country people go home for the weekend. They come back on Sunday because they have work first thing Monday morning.

"Like me, I suppose?" I said, thinking about my first job that I would be starting tomorrow.

"Well, not quite. You'll be living in Dublin now, so you won't have to get a train home, will you?"

"No, I suppose not." I smiled. "I didn't think you were coming," I said, changing the subject.

"Yeah, sorry about that. I bumped into an old friend and, well, you know how it is."

I knew exactly how it was. One friend insisted they go for a pint. The other agreed, partly because he did not want to cause offence and partly because he would have suggested it anyway had the other not said it first. And so it began, each man having to return the courtesy of buying the other a drink. A never-ending cycle that would only end when their money ran out, or when the landlord called time.

"That's all right, I've not waited long," I lied and, as always, kept my thoughts to myself. I wanted to shout at him, "*You selfish pig, sitting in a warm pub and not giving a damn about your poor niece, cold and alone in a strange city!*" But I never would...or never could? I pondered on the obvious difference between *never would* and *never could* for a moment before his hoarse voice intruded into my thoughts.

"We'll make a move so?" He reached down to pick up my case.

"Yes, okay," I said, and followed him toward the door, the same one where the tramp ranted and raved just minutes before. I hoped he would be long gone.

We walked out of the station and turned left, walking past a taxi rank where the drivers' faces peered out through steamed up windows. Peter passed the waiting taxis without looking at them and continued along the pavement toward a bus shelter. He walked fast and I was almost breaking into a jog as I attempted to keep pace with him. He marched straight past the bus stop where a young couple snogged while locked in each other's embrace, apparently oblivious to the world around them, or who might be watching their passionate cuddle.

We crossed a wide bridge and I saw the River Liffey for the first time. It was a cold and depressing image in the dark night, and a foul smell wafted up from the water below. A cold breeze blew down the river and froze my face as we made our way across. It was a relief to reach the other side where the walls of warehouses and derelict buildings bore the brunt of the wind.

"Is it far?" I asked Peter, who continued at the same pace without respite.

"Not too far."

We walked and walked, along cobblestoned streets and paved roads alike. It was late and men stumbled from pub doorways, turning their collars up before weaving a wavy path along the pavements.

Peter surged ahead while I struggled to keep up. The case seemed weightless in his strong arm and I reflected back to how I struggled to lift it both on and off the train.

"Peter!" I called ahead to him, and he stopped to wait for me. "Is it far?" I asked for the second time.

"Not too far now."

I wanted to say in a loud and sarcastic voice, "*you said that half an hour ago!*" But as is my habit, I did not express my thoughts, and continued to follow my uncle, who seemed to have no concept of distance.

Without the presence of moonlight, the streetlamps were the only source of light to guide our journey. They shone down, producing large orangey circles on the ground beneath them. We crossed well-lit roads peppered with Chinese takeaways and Italian chip shops. Their large windows oozed out light as if to guide customers to their doors. They made me think of lighthouses that shone out huge beams into the darkness. Other roads, much narrower and lined with houses on either side, were almost in blackness as they lacked the lampposts of the main roads. The only source of light on these roads was the dim glow that filtered through gaps in curtains.

I was ready to give up. My legs were at the point of buckling under me and my headed throbbed from a headache brought on by the freezing wind. My fingers were numb and had lost all sensation, and I tried to recall the symptoms of frostbite. Horrid pictures of blackened fingers and toes flashed into my mind. They were from a *National Geographic* magazine I once read while waiting in a doctor's surgery. If I recalled correctly, the blackened digits belonged to a polar explorer. I remember thinking they had been burnt, but after reading the article, I realised it was the result of frostbite and, as the flesh was dead, the only remedy was amputation. I shuddered, and not from the cold.

Just as I was contemplating on how I would manage to go through life with fingers and toes missing, we turned onto a side street. The street's name was displayed on a rusted wall plate fixed to a corner house. It read, "St Ignatius Road," and its faded lettering was just about visible in the half-light from a street lamp. I remembered the name. My mother told me this was the street where she was born and brought up on. It was one of the few things she told me about her life from before I was born. In fact, I had so few snippets of information that each piece was precious, and I memorized every one so as not to forget. I protected those memories as securely as one would safeguard the photographs of a departed loved one.

"We're here now," Peter said, confirming what I already knew.

"Which house is it?" I asked as I looked down the long, narrow street of terraced housing.

"It's there, halfway down on the left." He pointed as he spoke, but there was no great need to.

We walked past each house, window, door...window, door, window... The footpaths were narrow and two people would have difficulty walking abreast without stepping out onto the road. The houses had no gardens and should someone suddenly step out from a door, they would risk colliding with whoever happened to be walking passed at the time. Every window appeared to be covered with similar white lace curtains and in the dim light, it was impossible for me to distinguish between each house other than looking for the number upon each door.

"Here we are now," Peter announced as he stopped at number seventy-six, the house where my mother was born.

$\mathcal{T}wo$

Grandma hugged me and wept as her frail arms pulled me against her bosom. "You poor child, you poor child," she repeated over and over again.

For the first time since my mother died, I truly felt like an orphan, even more so than when I stood at the graveside that cold and wet morning five weeks earlier. I put my arms around her, but my embrace lacked strength. The truth was, although she was my mother's mother, she was still a stranger to me and I carried the embarrassment anyone would have when confronted with an emotional stranger. I had seen her face, though, many times. Mother kept an old biscuit tin on the top shelf of her wardrobe. Inside the tin were personal items of sentimental value to her. There were letters from my father, letters he wrote before the accident that took his life. Without her knowing, I read the letters. They gave me an insight into the father I had been too young to remember. He died tragically when I was just a baby. Included among the items was a solitary photograph of Grandma. It was taken a long time ago and her face, although similar, was that of a much younger woman.

She finally released me and I took a step backward, but she reached out to grip my cardigan sleeve with her thumb and forefinger and held on. It was as if she feared I would bolt out of the house in some desperate escape bid, but her light grasp would prevent any such notions from entering my head.

"You are the image of your mother," she said as a great sadness spread across her face and enveloped her. Her eyes grew heavy and reddened even more as fresh tears welled up and seeped over her eyelids to roll down her gaunt cheeks.

Looking into her old and sad eyes, I began to feel emotional myself. Without saying a word, I stepped forward and hugged her. This time, my grip was sincere and the bond of kinship had been confirmed. In that brief moment, she lost the persona of being a stranger to me.

Peter, who had been standing at the drawn curtains, coughed. It was a false cough, and I think he was tired of seeing two women crying and blubbing as sometimes we did. Grandma, taking the hint, straightened and composed herself at the same time.

"Where were you? We expected you hours ago. Was the train late? Did you get lost?" Her questions were thrown out with such rapidity that answering was impossible. She held her fingers to my cheek and said, "You poor child, you're frozen to the bone."

Before I could either comment or answer, she guided me toward an armchair next to the fireplace. As I sat down, I felt the heat on my legs and face. I held my hands close to the glowing heap of coals. My fingers had taken on a blue appearance, and they throbbed as the skin and bones absorbed the heat.

"Oh, Lord," Grandma said as the thought occurred to her. "You didn't walk from the station, did you?"

"Yes," I replied.

"But I gave money to Peter this morning for a taxi. Why did you not get a taxi?"

I did not know what to say and felt sure my look of confusion was plain to see, but her expression never altered. Her concerned eyes widened as she waited for me to reply. I looked to Peter for help.

"Yeah, sorry about that, Ma. I spent too much getting something to eat in town today. I only realised at the station I didn't have enough. We decided to walk and used what was left of the money to buy chips along the way."

I couldn't believe my ears and my jaw dropped open as a complete look of utter bewilderment enveloped my face. *You liar! You big, fat liar! You spent Grandma's money on booze and made your poor niece walk for miles in the freezing cold! And chips! What chips?* Of course, my rant that exposed his lies remained in my head and never left my lips, but surely,

Grandma would see through his falsehoods. One look at his red and bloated cheeks would reveal the truth. And if that was not enough, the stale stench of ale that refused to leave his breath and sat heavily in the room would betray him.

"Oh, that's a pity. Never mind, did you get a good meal?" she said to him with concern across her face that he might have gone hungry.

"It was okay," he said with an air of ungratefulness that she had paid for his meal, the meal that never existed.

She turned to me again and massaged my frozen fingers. "At least you got something warm to eat, Anna."

The fact that I was frozen to the point of numbness and had walked for miles through dark and bleak streets seemed of no concern anymore. I looked at him and caught his glance, but his face lacked shame. He looked from me to Grandma and back again. When his eyes met mine, I was astonished at the look of total innocence he displayed. He seemed to have no conception that I could so easily tear down his web of deceit if I decided to. Judging from the look of self-believed virtuousness, it seemed he would never in a million years think I would say anything to contradict him. And he wasn't far wrong. While the urge to speak up and set Grandma straight was great, I would not. Who was I to stir the pot? Me, an orphan that had just walked in the door.

"Where's Grandpa?" I asked, deciding to move on from the moment by changing the subject.

"He's gone to bed," she said.

"He always goes early," Peter said with a hint of sarcasm in his voice.

"Patrick likes to go to bed early and get up early. He says one hour before midnight is as good as two after," Grandma said, seemingly anxious to get the point across. She spoke as if trying to justify his absence, although there was no need as far as I was concerned. I was late arriving and would have hated to think he had upset his routine on my account.

"You must be exhausted, Anna," Grandma said.

"Yes, I am tired," I replied, my weariness evident in my voice.

The comfort of the armchair coupled with the fire's heat swept away the hype and excitement of the day, and exhaustion swept over me like an incoming wave. I was also hungry, but kept this fact to myself. After all, her money did treat Peter and me to a bag of hot chips during the walk from the station, or so she had been led to believe.

"What time do they want you at the hotel?" she asked.

"Not until twelve o'clock. It's just to show me my duties and sort me out with a uniform. I don't start actual work until Tuesday morning."

The hotel was, to be exact, The Royal Dublin Hotel, which I had been told was one of the most prestigious hotels in Dublin. However, my role there would be far less prestigious than the hotel's reputation. For I was going into service as a chambermaid. The term *chambermaid* was a little old fashioned for the 1950s. It summoned up images of old Victorian houses with the masters and ladies of the houses living in splendour while the chambermaid, snooty butler, and kitchen staff lived downstairs, only venturing upstairs when summoned to perform their housekeeping duties. But whether the term *chambermaid* or a more modern title such as *domestic worker* was used, it boiled down to the same thing—I was destined to spend my days cleaning rooms along with laundry duties, all while wearing the characteristic uniform of a chambermaid...sorry, domestic worker.

The position had been arranged by Mr Goodson who owned a small public house in our village. He did use the term *chambermaid* constantly. My mother had worked for him as a barmaid and, when things were quiet, a cleaner. He was a pleasant man and was fond of my mother, although not in a way that would be deemed inappropriate—he was, after all, three times her age. No, he simply liked my mother and appreciated the fact that she was someone who could be relied upon. After she died, he seemed to feel he had an inkling of responsibility for my welfare. Or maybe he just took pity on my situation, for I was near destitute.

Mother's savings amounted to a tidy sum of one thousand pounds, but her funeral was expensive and amounted to all but a few pounds of that money. Our rooms had been rented, and it was only due to the kind heart of our landlord that I was able to stay on rent-free for an extra month. Mr Goodson said he could not employ me because he was intending to retire and pass the business on to his eldest son and his wife. And so it was arranged through a friend of his in the hotel industry that the position of a domestic worker was procured for me.

It was not my wish to do such work, but as the saying went, beggars can't be choosers, and I was for all intents and purposes, a beggar. For without means, I relied on the charity of others. Not that I was ungrateful. I owed a debt of thanks to both Mr Goodson and our landlord. Their charity found a place in my heart, which would never be forgotten.

It came to be that I found myself at my grandparents' house that night. I knew no one else in Dublin and, being broke, I had no money for lodgings. I wrote to Grandma, explaining my situation. I also mentioned I was aware of the fact that my mother had not been in contact with them for many years, the reason for which I was unsure of, as she made a point never to discuss them. I stressed that if I was not welcome or if they were unable to accommodate me, then no answer was necessary and I would harbour no ill feelings as to their decision.

But, I did receive a reply within a week of posting my letter. Grandma's written words could not have been more welcoming as to my staying with them. Her letter flowed with comments such as, *God has answered my prayers,* and *my heart awaits you, poor child.* It was a genuine outpouring of transcribed emotion, and her sentiments moved me.

My bedroom reminded me of an igloo, although, I admit to never spending a night in an igloo. The temperature was freezing, and whirling plumes of vapour rose into the cold air each time I exhaled. Had there been a breeze, the wind chill would have frozen me solid. There was a small fireplace, but the bed had been pushed up against it, making it unusable. The bed could not be moved as it took up most of the room, leaving only a small gap between it and the wall, just enough for me to squeeze my way along after coming in through the door. I realised then, the front bedroom had been split in two with a partition wall—Peter's room being on the other side. There was no space for a wardrobe or side-press, so my belongings would have to remain in the case and stored beneath the bed.

The window was covered with a flimsy curtain that did little to keep out the cold. Despite the bed filling the room, the most dominant feature was a large wooden cross fixed to the wall above the top of the bed. My first thought upon seeing it was to hope a sturdy nail had been driven into the plaster, for if it fell while I slept...I might never wake up. We had never been religious and the image of this imposing cross sent a shiver down my spine. It was not so much the religious connotations, rather it was because the room was so bare of personal items, the cross seemed to dominate everything as it looked down on me. For a brief moment, I felt as if I had entered a convent and this was to be my cell. It was stripped of everything to reflect my discarding of all possessions as I gave myself to the Great Almighty—not that I possessed anything of value to discard, but the feeling was there.

I changed into my nightdress, but after slipping between the ice-cold sheets, I was soon rummaging in my case for my cardigan and socks. Wrapped up in bulky clothes, I settled down to spend my first night in Dublin.

Three

If Grandma made me feel like an orphan taken in and showered with love, my first meeting with Grandpa had the complete opposite effect. I left the house that first morning with the feeling I was a stray dog that had wandered into the house of Patrick O'Brien. An unwanted dog at that, and one which would only be housed and fed on the clear understanding that the mangy cur pay its way in whatever fashion the master of the house saw fit.

I slept late as my body ebbed away the mental and physical exertions of the previous day. It was ten o'clock when I got up. Grandma had already left for her job at the laundry shop. Peter was still in bed, and his snoring resonated throughout the house. I made my way down to the kitchen and found Grandpa sitting at the table reading the morning paper.

"Grandpa?" I said, knowing it was him, but as he did not speak when I entered, it was the only thing I could think of saying to break the uncomfortable silence.

He closed and folded his newspaper, taking meticulous care not to create any new creases. "So, you've arrived," he said, his stone-cold face staring at me with an intenseness that made me instantly apprehensive.

"Y-Yes," I said, stuttering as I answered. It was something I had never done before.

"Don't you have a job to go to?" he muttered without altering his expression.

I was astounded by his lack of emotion and found it difficult to speak for a few moments. His entire manner was cold, from his hardened expression to his abrupt sentences.

"Yes, but not until twelve o'clock," I finally said.

"I suppose you will be wanting breakfast?"

I did not know what to say. My mouth opened, but no words came out. It was his first time to meet his granddaughter and even the basic courtesies of, *hello* and *how are you* were not forthcoming.

"There's bread in the tin and porridge in the press. You will have to boil water if you want tea."

"Just bread will be fine, thank you," I said, finally pulling myself together to some small degree. I thanked him as a vagrant might thank a faceless stranger that tossed a coin into the unfortunate's begging bowl. I sat down to eat my bread in silence, and his attention went back to his newspaper. The atmosphere could have been cut with a knife, and I hoped Peter might appear and relieve my suffering, but the loud snores from his room continued to echo through the house.

"He won't fall out of bed until the afternoon," he said, apparently reading my thoughts.

"Grandma said he would walk me to work."

"Huh." He grunted. "You can't rely on that layabout...useless sod." He uttered the end of his sentence with emphasised venom in his voice.

The deafening silence returned, and when the uncomfortable situation became unbearable, I stood up to wash my plate in the sink, eager to be on my way and to leave his presence.

"I'll tell you how to get there," he said in an air that indicated I was putting him to great inconvenience rather than the pleasant tone people used when they were glad to be of help.

After Grandpa gave me directions to the Royal Dublin, he said something else that utterly astounded and embarrassed me.

"You'll be obliged to hand up half your pay for room and board. We are not that well-off that we can afford to feed extra mouths, even if they are related."

I was shocked and did my best to hide my astonishment, but I fear my reddening cheeks betrayed me. I agreed and left as quickly as I could, relieved to be away from him. I had no objection to paying my way. In fact, I would have insisted on paying for my keep, as that was only fair. It was the way he put it to me, the lack of emotion in his voice, his abrupt manner, and his apparent dislike of me. As I pulled the front door closed behind me, I consoled myself with the thought that Grandma would be home when I returned.

Dublin had taken on a completely new atmosphere in the light of day. As instructed, I turned right at the end of the road and walked along Dorset Street. Small shops sold their wares and some had stock laid out on the footpath to attract business from passersby. A continuous throng of people went in and out of doorways as they made their way from one shop to another. There were shops of every kind and I kept pausing to look in windows as I passed. I was always intrigued at how passing different shops affected one's senses, depending on the type of store it was. I stood outside a bakery shop and the sweet aroma of freshly baked bread filled my nostrils. At the same time, the heat of the ovens created an invisible warm glow that reached out and embraced me in the doorway. I lingered there for a few moments, basking in its heat. In stark contrast, the next store was a butcher shop, and the whitewashed walls along with the sawdust-covered floor filled me with a feeling of coldness.

Dorset Street was a main road into the city centre and buses and cars jostled one another for space in the narrow lanes. When it came time for me to cross, I was hesitant to pass between the traffic, even though it had slowed to a crawl. I was not used to such congestion on a road. Our country village had so few cars that in any one hour, one could have counted the passing vehicles on the fingers of one hand. The drivers of those cars and vans would almost always wave a hand in a gesture of friendliness, regardless of whether you knew them or not. But in the city, it was so different. Drivers sat stony-faced, staring blankly at the rear of the vehicle in front of them, their knuckles white from grasping steering wheels.

I watched others crossing and they were practically fearless of the traffic. I selected a pedestrian that was walking toward the curb. He was a tall man wearing a long, black leather coat that swished around his ankles. He carried a foil wrapped lunch in one hand and had a paper tucked under his other arm. As he stepped into the road, I rushed forward to cross at his side. He walked briskly, his long legs taking naturally extended strides. I had to jog as I kept pace with him. We reached the opposite side safely and went our separate ways. I watched him walk into the distance, oblivious to how he had guided a country girl safely across her first busy urban street.

The walk to the hotel took thirty minutes, twice the length of time I spent there. I was brought into the office and asked to fill out some forms. Name...address...next of kin. *Next of kin?* Just routine, they assured me. My job proper was to start at seven a.m. the following day, and one of the other girls would show me the ropes, so to speak.

Before I knew where I was, I found myself wandering across O'Connell Street with the rest of the afternoon to kill. I had no money for lunch or even to buy a cup of tea and had to endure walking past cafe windows where customers sat eating and drinking with no comprehension of how lucky they were. I considered going home, but quickly dispelled that notion. The thought of facing Grandpa again caused a knot to well up in my stomach. No, I decided I would wait until teatime when Grandma would be there.

So off I went to explore the city on my own. I marvelled at the large department store windows along Dublin's main street and recoiled upon seeing the prices of the clothes on display. They were beautiful, and seeing my reflection in a window, I felt like a pauper. My coat was a size too small and my light blue cardigan was only that faded colour from two years of washing. When it was new, it was a good few shades darker than its present shade. I looked down at my skirt and saw loose threads dangling from the hem, flittering in the wind. *Someday*, I thought. *Someday, I'll be able to wander the shop floors, picking out whatever takes my fancy, and not even bother to check the prices.* Well, a girl could dream, could she not?

I crossed the grey flowing waters of the Liffey by the Ha'penny Bridge. The walkway was narrow and the people mashed together as they tried to pass one another. The noise underfoot of boots and shoes prodding the wooden planks sounded like a badly trained army marching across a drawbridge. Halfway across, a Traveller woman sat, her folded legs covered with a blanket. In one arm, she rocked a baby, holding the infant's bare head close to her bosom. The other hand grasped a paper cup and she held it out, pleading for pennies from the crowd, who did their best not to make eye contact with the dishevelled beggar. I studied her weather-beaten face and felt pity for the woman who had aged far quicker than any woman should. She turned toward me and, to my shame, I looked away as so many had done before me, for I had nothing to give.

I continued to walk without any idea of where I was or where I was going. I wandered around stores to get in out of the cold more than to actually view the goods on sale. An eager sales clerk practically accosted me in a furniture store. I was looking at a settee and could not resist the temptation to sit down. The extravagant comfort was pure luxury as I sank deep into the soft cushions. He tried everything possible to talk me into purchasing it. In an effort to rid myself of him, I said the colour was not ideal and would clash with other furnishings. Poppycock, of course—the make-believe furnishings only existed in my make-believe house.

"No problem, miss," he said. "We can have the settee covered in any colour fabric that suits you."

Having failed with the colour clash idea, I tried another approach. "It might be too large for our sitting room," I said in my best la-de-da accent.

"You're in luck, miss. We also do have the same settee in a two-seater version," he said enthusiastically.

He was pushing enthusiasm over that fine line that divides eagerness and annoying persistence, but I still did not have the heart to tell him I wasn't interested. After all, if I couldn't afford a cup of tea, I could hardly afford an Italian designed settee.

"I do like it," I said. "But I'll have to bring my father in to see it first."

Eureka, it worked, although I was left feeling as if I had burst a child's balloon. His face lost all friendliness as he backed away. I guess he had heard the line or similar words to the same effect many times before.

It was early evening when I retraced my steps back

down Dorset Street. Most of the small shops that lined both sides of the road had closed. I passed darkened windows and graffiti-covered shutters as late autumn leaves fluttered past, blown by a sharp, cold breeze.

Seventy-six Ignatius Road stood nestled between two similar terraced houses, and as I approached the door, I lacked the warm feeling of relief normally experienced when returning home on a cold, dark evening. I knocked on the door.

"Anna," Grandma said, welcoming me with a warm smile. "Come in, child, I've been waiting for you to come home."

She was alone in the house and brought me into the kitchen where the heat of the stove warmed the whole room. A white linen tablecloth covered the kitchen table, its edges finely decorated with an intricate lace pattern. A place was set and Grandma fussed over me as if I were a guest of honour.

"Is Peter not home?" I asked.

"No, he's gone out."

"And Grandpa?" I said.

"He's at the Workers' Club. He goes most nights."

"What's a Workers' Club?" I asked.

Her eyes turned upward. "Just another name for a public house. He thinks because it's a club restricted to *members* only, it can't be classed as boozing. He condemns Peter for going to the pub too often, yet he goes to his workers' club all the time. There's hypocrisy for you, don't you think?"

I smiled but remained silent. I wanted to agree and back up her condemnations of Grandpa with comments such as *the pot calling the kettle black*. I mean, she practically invited me to say something negative. But I said nothing, letting my smile answer the question.

I went to bed, as I had an early start in the morning. Twice I was awakened from my sleep. The first time was when Grandpa came home. I heard the front door being pulled shut and the noise of his heavy footsteps on the wooden stairs. The second time was when Peter came home. Even before I glanced at the clock, I knew it was an ungodly hour. His footsteps on the stairs were confused. It was as if his feet dragged and he took two steps back for every one forward. The silence of the night seemed to exaggerate every noise he made. I could hear him stumbling around his room for quite a while before he decided to go to bed. His bedsprings creaked in protest when he fell onto the mattress. Then there was a sudden silence and the quietness of the early hour once more asserted itself.

I closed my eyes and drifted back to sleep. But it was not a contented sleep, for I dreamt sad dreams peppered with visions of my mother. She was calling to me, warning me of what I did not know, for her words were distant and indefinable.

Four

I felt as if I had walked into another world—a world of luxury and grandeur. A great chandelier hung above the main foyer and its delicate glass droplets sparkled magnificently against the dark oak ceiling beams. A roaring fire blazed in a large fireplace, which was enclosed by a smooth white marble surround. Although sitting some twenty feet away, I could feel the intense heat emitted from the dancing flames as they appeared to be sucked upwards into the chimney shaft. When the receptionist called me, I stood, and my feet seemed to sink into the deep folds of the carpet as I walked toward her.

"Anna, this is Rebecca," the receptionist said, glancing to a girl standing at the end of the desk. "You'll be working with her today and she'll help you with anything you need."

Rebecca smiled, and I returned her smile in acknowledgement of her wordless but friendly welcome. She was a slim girl and a little taller than me. Her most noticeable feature was her face. Her skin was smooth like silk and without the slightest blemish. She wore no makeup and her natural beauty seemed to excel because of it. I guessed she was a few years older than me. Even in her uniform, her exquisite figure showed more curves than I could ever hope for myself. When she turned, her auburn hair swished around with elegant style and reminded me of autumn-coloured trees swaying back and forth before the wind.

I followed Rebecca down a backstairs that led to the staff changing rooms. The dim corridors and narrow stairwells lacked the sophisticated charm of the hotel. Used for staff only, they were bare of carpets, and the whitewashed walls were marked with black scuffmarks at every turn.

"Where are you from?" she asked.

"County Sligo...and you?"

"Cork, originally, but I've been in Dublin since I was five or six." Her voice was sweet and without any hint of a Cork accent.

Following Rebecca's lead, I sat on one of the benches to chat. She seemed in no great hurry to put me to work and I was glad, trying to use the time to calm my nerves and settle into my new surroundings.

"Why did your family move to Dublin?" I asked.

"Ah no, I don't have any family—"

"Oh, I'm sorry," I interrupted, feeling dreadfully embarrassed, for what exact reason I did not know.

"You're grand," she said, her voice taking on a more pronounced Dublin accent. "I grew up in an orphanage. They moved me to Dublin when I was young. I'm not sure why. Lack of space in Cork, I suppose."

"Have you worked here long?" I asked, trying to get away from the subject, although, it was me that seemed to carry the embarrassment. Rebecca was completely unfazed by the topic.

"Three years," she said, rolling her eyes upward as she did. "When I was seventeen, the nuns told me they were no longer responsible for my welfare, but they were kind enough to organise a grotty bedsit on Gardiner Street and a glamorous job in one of Ireland's most prestigious hotels." She held out her hands to signify the hotel and her smile slowly gave way to a giggle, and then a fit of laughter.

I could not help but follow. Despite the obvious sadness of her story, she possessed the wonderful attribute of natural humour. We finally stopped laughing and managed to regain control of ourselves, but from that moment on, the slightest thing could cause us to giggle uncontrollably.

Rebecca opened a large wooden cabinet and along the metal rail hung new uniforms, still wrapped in their protective polythene covers. She helped me find one that fit and the scene began to resemble a fashion show. Encouraged by Rebecca, I paraded around the changing room, kitted out in the guise of a hotel cleaner, as she preferred to refer to the job title.

At first, I was embarrassed and, for a brief moment, wondered if she was making fun of me. I was not pretty like her. I knew that and was under no illusions about the fact. Nobody ever told me I was pretty. Well, that's not quite true, my mother did, and quite often. But don't all mothers tell their daughters they are pretty? It went with the job. I could have had a third ear growing in the centre of my forehead and my mother would still have said, "*you are so pretty, just like a princess.*" Of course, all daughters are princesses to their parents and those same parents are blinded by love, but the darling princesses are not blinded by love. We can look in the mirror and see the truth. We can't all be pretty. Some of us have to settle for plain or even ugly. Not that I considered myself ugly. I didn't, but I was no fool. I was small, ordinary, and just plain Anna.

When I looked at Rebecca, she was smiling. Smiles could be deceptive, but the eyes never lied. I'd been told you could read a person by their body language. By the way they crossed their legs, or maybe the way they rubbed their chin. Did they have to rub their chin? Or was that a tell-tale sign that they were uncomfortable, hiding their emotions, showing the involuntary movements after telling an untruth. But the eyes never lied. A lot could be gained by looking into someone's eyes, those two portals into the human soul. And Rebecca's eyes? They were smiling, just as she was, and I knew in that instant, she was sincere.

The rest of the morning was spent cleaning rooms, and I came to realise just how monotonous the work was going to be. Every room required the same repetitive actions. Change the bedclothes, replace used towels, clean the toilet, empty the bin, and sweep the carpet if need be. We pushed a cart laden down with towels, sheets, and cleaning utensils. From room to room and floor to floor, we worked our way from top to bottom. Half the rooms were not in use, but Rebecca told me that on holiday weekends and right through the summer months, every room would be occupied and need cleaning.

There were perks, or rather *a* perk to the job. At dinner-time, Rebecca brought me down to the kitchen, where Rodrigo, the hotel chef, fed us the most glorious meal. Actually, it was only Shepherd's Pie, but after a hard morning of cleaning and being surrounded by the heat of the ovens, and the aroma of freshly cooked food, my meal seemed to have an enhanced taste to it.

We finished work at five o'clock and walked home together. It was only a ten-minute stroll to where she lived. We parted at the front door of the house where her flat was, on the top floor overlooking Mountjoy Square, which was across the road. We hugged as if we had been friends all our lives and I promised to call for her in the morning. To my delight, she suggested we walk to and from work together every day.

I cut through the enclosed square before making my way to Dorset Street. The park was quiet as I walked across the wet lawns. The playground was empty, too dark and too cold for children to venture out. A small dog ran wild and an old man clapped his hands and shouted its name. His cries were in vain as the dog, glad to be free of the lead, ignored his master and continued to run as if trying to burn up the excitement within him.

As I passed close to the man, I saw his eyes roll up to the heavens and a silent barrage of anger and obscenities in his muttering lips. I feared for the dog and what punishment he would receive at the hands of his furious owner—a smack on the nose, or maybe something worse? I stopped at the far gate and looked back across the park. I was relieved to see the dog had returned to him and the old man was kneeling, furiously rubbing the dog, whose tail was whipping left and right so fast it was just a blur.

When I got home, everybody was there. Grandpa crouched over the fireplace, stoking the burning coal as if trying to encourage the smouldering nuggets to give a last surge of heat before they frizzled away to ash. Peter sat watching the television, although the sound was turned down and the picture rolled with bad reception. He had a bottle of beer in his hand, and another two empty ones lay discarded on the floor.

"Hello, niece!" he called from his chair.

"Hello, Peter. Hello, Grandpa."

Grandpa turned his head half toward me and grunted something incoherent, as if begrudgingly being forced to acknowledge my presence. But Peter's welcome was as warm as a welcome could be, even if it was alcohol fuelled as he raised his bottle with a big smile to toast my arrival.

Grandma welcomed me with a kiss on the cheek and produced a bowl of Irish stew, which she placed on the kitchen table.

"How was your first day at work?" she asked as she sat down to face me.

"Good," I said.

And it was good, I thought to myself. I had decided the work was going to be bearable. The hotel was nice and everyone was pleasant to me. I was allowed to eat in the kitchen and I had met Rebecca. From the moment we met, we *clicked,* as they say. Rebecca was funny, honest, and pretty, all rolled up in the one package. I had made my first friend in Dublin and I hoped she looked on me in the same light.

I told Grandma I could get free meals in the hotel and she wouldn't have to cook for me. I thought she would be pleased as it did not seem fair for her to cook after her day's work, but I was mistaken. A look of sadness swept across her face and she went quiet, unnaturally quiet. I realised then that she wanted to cook for me, to look after me, to keep me safe...to mother me. And what had I done? I said I did not need her. At least that's the way she was reading it.

"Of course, Grandma," I said, trying to recover lost ground. "I do get one day off a week and, even on the days I do work, I could do with something small in the evenings."

It worked. Her face regained a hint of happiness as she smiled in recognition of her duties. She began to list the types of food she would prepare in the evenings. I remained silent, even as I realised the snacks she would prepare would be of equivalent size to the dinners they would be replacing.

$\mathcal{F}ive$

It is said that nothing passes faster than time, and I was inclined to agree with that maxim. Without really noticing the days passing by, I found I had been living in Dublin for a full month. The first few weeks had not been easy. Settling into my new home was difficult. Grandma was wonderful and Peter, God bless him, was a harmless if somewhat misguided soul. My difficulties lay with Grandpa. He had barely spoken more than a few words to me since my arrival, and those words he did speak were usually preceded and followed by grunts or similar snorts of apparent disapproval. He treated Grandma and Peter with much the same discourtesy, but in my case, it seemed to go beyond plain rudeness. I believed he harboured a deep-seated dislike for me. For what reason, I did not know, and as yet, I felt uncomfortable bringing up the subject with Grandma.

Avoiding him would have seemed impossible in such a small house, but luckily, my hours at the hotel helped to facilitate my desire to evade his company. I left early, as the dusty rays of the dawn sunlight were just beginning to creep over the terraced rooftops. When I returned in the evening, he would already be gone to his beloved Workers' Club. And with luck, I would be asleep when he returned, as I was going to bed early every night.

But after a month of the same day in, day out routine, I was not as weary in the evenings as I had been at first. I seemed to be less tired as my body got used to the long days. Indeed, I was aware of the change within myself. I was beginning to find a renewed energy in the evenings. Despite the fact I was going to bed at a later hour, more often than not, I would be awake even before the alarm clock began to rattle annoyingly on the floor the following morning. The drawback to going to bed at a later hour was that I risked being up when Grandpa returned from the club. His humour was not enhanced by alcohol, and the influence of drink appeared only to solidify his impoliteness. As long as Grandma was present, I felt safe. She acted as a barrier against his verbal boorishness, taking the brunt of it herself with a certain amount of indifference.

I'd bonded with Rebecca in a way I never had with anyone. I had friends before, but never real friends in the sense I could say or do anything without fear of ridicule or reproach. She had a unique personality that invited openness, at least from me. It was as if honesty was the moth and she was the light. We talked and talked, oh how we talked. In the few short weeks of our friendship, we came to know every single thing there was to know about each another. I told her secrets I never dreamed of divulging to another living being, and after I did, it felt good. To unburden one's heart to a friend was a truly rewarding experience.

One morning while I was busy cleaning one of the second floor rooms, Rebecca came rushing down the corridor in search of me. Before she uttered a word, I read the excitement in her face. It was the face of a child upon discovering presents under the Christmas tree. Her cheeks were red and her eyes widened to such a degree I would almost have thought it impossible. And her smile, oh what a smile it was, fuelled by delight.

"What's happened?" I asked.

She could not speak for a few moments as she huffed and puffed, trying to control her breathing.

"He's coming!" she finally blurted out.

"Who's coming?"

"My Frenchman, Mr Beaufort, that's who."

"Who is Mr Beaufort?"

"He's a regular guest. Oh he's gorgeous, Anna, just you

wait until you see him."

"How do you know he is coming?"

"I saw it in the reservations book. He's booked in from the twenty-third to the twenty-ninth. A whole week!"

"That's wonderful," I said, hoping she would not detect the lack of enthusiasm in my voice. Why was I not happy for her? I wanted to see her find happiness, but something told me it would not be with this man. I was not untrusting by nature, quite the opposite, but a doubt about this man, a man I had yet to meet, gnawed away inside of me.

"I bet he asks me out this time," she said, her voice trembling with anticipation.

"What makes you think he will?"

"I don't know, but if you had seen the way he looked at me last time he was here, then you'd understand."

Our conversation ended abruptly when we heard the voice of Mr Wilkinson, the hotel manager, farther down the hall. Rebecca grabbed a tin of polish from my trolley to use as a pretense for her presence before turning to return upstairs.

"We'll talk later." These were her parting words as she hurried away.

We did talk later. Rebecca invited me to her flat and I agreed to call at eight o'clock. It was my first time visiting her place. She lived on the top floor of the tenement building, which had flats on every floor. Even with the hall lights on, the stairs leading up to the fourth floor was shrouded in a depressing dimness. The carpet was a dark blue colour and blackened from decades of traipsing feet that trudged up and down the creaking stairs. While the dirty carpets did little to reflect the dim light, the walls achieved even less—a dull purplish colour of thick paint covering every wall from top to bottom.

I brought tea, biscuits, and cake. We enjoyed our small feast, sitting cross-legged and close to the small fireplace that was the room's only source of heat. Tiny orange sparks leapt both up and outwards as the damp sticks hissed and crackled in the hearth.

"Do you know anything about this Mr Beaufort?" I asked, careful that my tone did not sound patronising or mocking.

"Not much really," she said, her face illuminating with the mere thought of him. "He works for some big international company and travels all over Europe. Just imagine, Anna, the Riviera, Rome, Spain." She reached out to grasp my hand before continuing. "All the places I can only dream about."

"And Dublin, of course," I said.

"Yes, Dublin, every month or so, but who wants to be in dreary Dublin when you can drink coffee in a French cafe with the Eiffel Tower dominating the city skyline, or feel the warmth of the Mediterranean sun on your bare skin whilst sitting on a Spanish beach?"

"You think he might whisk you away to those places?" I tried to conceal my concerns in my tone, but I failed. Whether she detected doubt in my voice or read my facial expressions, I do not know, but she did pick up something and became defensive.

"I don't see why not. He's not married and I know he likes me. You have never met him or even seen him for that matter, so please don't treat me as foolish. I'm not a naive schoolgirl, you know."

"I'm sorry," I said, upset I'd opened a rift between us and our first words of tension had been uttered. "You're right, of course, I've never met him. It's just that it's so fantastic, the handsome stranger whisking the poor girl away to wine and dine her in the world's finest restaurants. It's the stuff of fairy tales really."

Rebecca laughed and said, "Jesus, you're making me sound like Cinderella."

The tense moment passed and we laughed at her comparison to a fairy tale princess. From that moment on, I realised I would have to tread carefully when it came to the subject of Mr Beaufort.

It was late when I returned home. Grandma was still up and sitting in the kitchen. The house was quiet and she had a worried expression.

"I'm sorry I'm so late, Grandma, you shouldn't have waited up."

"Oh, Anna. I'm worried about Peter."

"Why?"

"He had an argument with your grandfather this morning. He stormed out in an awful temper."

"I'm sure he will be alright, Grandma. He is a grown man."

She didn't answer.

"You should go to bed, Grandma. You have to get up early for work in the morning."

"I won't be able to sleep, not until I know he's home and safe."

There was an awkward moment of silence. I was tired and wanted to sleep, but her worried expression made it impossible for me to leave her.

"Do you have any idea where he went?"

"I think he went to Quinn's Bar in Drumcondra." She looked at me, her eyes asking the unspoken question.

"Do you want me to bring him home?"

"Oh, Anna, will you?"

"Yes, of course," I said, silently cursing Peter in my mind. But for Grandma, I would do it.

Six

A misty rainfall began as I walked to Quinn's public house in Drumcondra. It was only a short distance, but before I got even halfway, the fog-like vapour penetrated my clothes, leaving me cold and wet to the point where I felt truly miserable.

Peter was not hard to find. As soon as I stepped in the door, I saw him through the thick haze of stale cigarette smoke that hung in the air like a stagnant cloud. He was sitting at the bar, alone and hunched forward, peering mournfully into a half-empty glass of stout.

"Hello, Peter," I said, squeezing myself between two bar stools.

"Anna!" He spoke loudly and a warm smile spread across his face. He straightened his posture, as if that action alone would sweep away his depression.

"Grandma sent me, she's worried about you."

"Will you have a drink?" he asked, looking around to get the attention of the bartender.

"No, thank you. I think we should go home."

"Ah come on, have a drink with your Uncle Peter. I've been on my own all day." He waved to the bartender, having no intention of accepting my refusal. "Another one for me, and Anna, what will you have?"

"Just a mineral," I said, giving in to his insistence.

"A mineral?" he asked in disbelief, looking at me as if I had committed a mortal sin.

"I don't drink," I said. That was actually a small lie. I'd

drunk and would no doubt do so again, but the last thing I wanted at that moment was to present him with a drinking buddy.

"Alright," he said, shrugging before turning to the bartender and asking him to get me a glass of red lemonade.

"Can we sit somewhere else?" I said.

"Why? What's wrong with here?" he asked with a genuine look of confusion.

I looked around the bar before answering. There were ten or fifteen men, no women. All of them were old like Grandpa and most were bundled up in heavy coats and wearing tweed caps. Even Peter looked out of place here, although he could never see it. "I'd just feel more comfortable in the lounge," I finally said, still looking around as I spoke.

Without uttering a word, he stood, picked up our glasses, and led me across the bar and through a glass-panelled door into the lounge. I instantly felt more comfortable in our new surroundings. The room was brighter than the bar and at least three times as big. Barely half the tables were occupied, but the customers were of a younger generation. I no longer felt the self-consciousness of being the only female as the gender balance was roughly even.

We sat in the far corner. I watched as Peter took large gulps from his glass. An immense glee of satisfaction spread across his face with every taste of the black ale.

"So, what are you doing here, little niece?" he asked, his voice slightly slurred, although I expected him to be in a far worse state considering he had spent the entire day in the pub.

"I told you, Grandma was worried and she asked me to bring you home."

"I'm not going home while that grumpy bastard is there."

"You mean Grandpa?"

"Who else? And don't say you disagree with me. I've noticed how you try to avoid him, going to bed early and running a mile when you hear his voice."

"I don't think he likes me," I said, realising this might be an opportunity to get some answers.

"He doesn't, but don't take it personally, because he doesn't like the rest of us either."

"Surely not. You're angry, Peter." I tried to convince him he was wrong, but in the back of my mind, I wasn't so sure.

"Of course he does, the cantankerous git."

"But why?" I asked.

"I don't know. I know I'm not much use, but I've never done anything really bad, and Mother, well, what has she done? Only spend her life skiving for him."

I sat back in the chair and took a sip of my lemonade. It was cold and two ice cubes bobbed around the top of the glass, making small clinking noises. "I can't believe he hates Grandma, I just can't."

"Well why else does he treat her the way he does?" he said.

"What do you mean?"

"The way he talks to her. Surely you've noticed? And making her work at her age—"

"Making her work?" I interrupted.

"Sure. He enjoys his days now he's retired while she slaves away in that laundry shop."

"Does she have to work?" I asked. I never put much thought into it, but I assumed she wanted to be doing something while Grandpa preferred to enjoy his retirement at home.

Peter laughed mockingly, although I sensed his derision was not aimed at me.

"You have no idea, do you? But I suppose, how could you know?"

"Know what?" I said.

"When Dad retired, he got a decent pension, along with a very nice lump sum. And do you know what he did?" He leaned back, tasting his ale, apparently waiting for me to hazard a guess.

"No, how would I?"

"No," he said. "How would you?" He put his glass down with a thump on the table and the ale splashed over the rim. "Well, I'll tell you, little niece. I'm going to tell you what a miserable bastard he really is."

I waited for him to continue, a little shocked that someone could talk so disparagingly about one of their parents.

"Like I said," he continued, "he got a tidy sum on his retirement, along with a silver watch on a chain, which he keeps tucked away still in its case. 'Too good to wear,' he says. When he came home after his last day at work, he bought Mother one of those new washing machines as a present. When she asked about the pension, he put his finger to his nose to tell her that was his business and not hers. As far as he was concerned, he'd worked all his life and that was his money. And that was that, end of discussion."

"So, he gives her nothing?"

"Well, not nothing. He gives her a few pound every week, just enough to cover his food and little else. Even the money you leave for him every week, Mother sees none of it. It goes into his pocket. That's why she works, to make a few extra pounds to survive, not because she enjoys slaving away at her age."

"That doesn't seem fair," I said.

"It's not. He forgets, or rather chooses to forget, that while all those years he spent going to work, she kept the house, cooked his meals, washed his clothes, and reared his children. Nope, it's not fair at all. That pension rightly belongs to the both of them, but he doesn't see it that way."

To say that Peter's revelations shocked me would be a titanic understatement. As early as my second day in the city, I had decided I did not like Grandpa. His rudeness and apparent dislike of me assured that. But this new insight into the man's meanness turned my dislike into a loathing. Grandma's sweet face flashed into my mind and his treatment of her utterly disgusted me.

Peter, despite his verbal assassination of his father, was in a good mood, thanks to the many pints of ale he had drunk over the day. I realised it was my chance to find out the details of why Grandpa seemed to despise me. Details I knew I could never ask Grandma about, and I would never dare to broach the subject with Grandpa. I brought up the topic in a roundabout way in case he would have problems discussing it, but I need not have feared, as he was quite forthcoming in his own blunt way.

"You remind him of Maria, that's the reason. She's gone now, so he has transferred his hate onto you."

I was taken aback and took a deep breath before saying anything. "He hated my mother, his own daughter, but why?"

"It's because of you," he said. "You mean you really don't know?"

"Me? What have I done?" I asked, confused.

"You were born, that's your crime, at least it is in his eyes. And it's one that will never be forgiven, not by him anyway." Peter tilted his head back and drained the end of his drink. He signalled the bartender for another.

I was lost for words. A sickening pang developed in my stomach. It was as if I had just committed a hideous crime and was waiting to be found out. And as the horrible deed had been done, there was nothing I could do except wait for my punishment. I composed myself as Peter tasted a fresh pint of Guinness that was placed on the table.

"Tell me, Peter. Tell me why my presence is so reviled by him."

He remained quiet, and I could tell he was having second thoughts about continuing. But, I had to know. Peter was the only one that could be so easily forthcoming with information. I decided to play on his weaknesses, which might not be ethical, but my desire to find out the truth was stronger than any qualms I had about pulling the right strings.

"Would you like another drink, Peter?" I added, "My treat."

"Sure." His face lit up with the prospect of someone else paying.

The bartender came over and I asked for two drinks—a pint of ale, and a glass of wine for myself.

"I thought you didn't drink?" he said as the bartender walked away.

"Well, hardly ever. I just feel like something stronger than lemonade."

"Welcome to my world, little niece," he said, reaching out to pat me sympathetically on the shoulder.

In the space of a few seconds, I had dispelled any inhibitions he had about continuing. Men always talked more freely to drinking buddies, everybody knew that, and that was what I had become when I ordered the drinks. Not only that, but my request for something stronger created a bond of sorts between us in his simple line of thought. I had made a formal declaration that I was on his side in the cold war against Grandpa.

Our drinks came and I felt a warm sensation as the wine went down. Peter gulped some of his fresh pint and sighed with approving satisfaction before using the back of his hand to wipe away a foamy white moustache above his upper lip.

"Tell me about the time my mother left. She never told

me anything about it."

"I don't know much, I was only a kid, about eight or nine. Maria was ten years older than me."

"You must remember something," I said, placing my hand on his arm "Anything at all?"

He pursed his lips, blowing out a steady stream of breath as he taxed his memory. "Maria was strong-willed, I do remember that. Her and Da were always fighting. She wasn't afraid of him, you see, and had no problem in speaking her mind. Of course, he didn't like that, someone standing up to him, I mean."

"Is that why she left?"

"No, not quite, there was more to her leaving than that," he said.

"How do you mean?"

"To be honest, I didn't understand at the time. It was only as I got older that I really understood what happened."

"And what was that, Peter?"

He withdrew into himself for a few moments. I waited for him to continue, but he was saying nothing, so I realised I would have to push him a bit.

"Peter, you have to tell me. Whatever it is, it's no worse than leaving me wondering and not knowing. Not after coming this far. Please tell me. Please!"

"Well, I suppose you have a right to know," he said.

I nodded and my lips pressed together as I waited for him to continue.

"Like I said, I was just a kid, but something happened and they were arguing a lot more than usual. I remember being in my bedroom and listening to their raised voices through the floor. I couldn't help but hear, as they were yelling really loud."

"What was the argument about?" I asked.

"I didn't know then, but Dad was shouting and calling Maria 'a dirty slag' and Ma was in the background saying, 'It wasn't her fault.' I can't remember what Maria was saying, but she was crying a lot."

"What happened next? Can you remember?"

"Not really. It's all a bit vague. All I know is when I woke the next morning, Maria was gone. Da acted like she never existed, wouldn't even say her name. Ma was upset. She cried a lot and refused to talk to the git for weeks afterwards."

I finished my wine. Peter did not want another drink. His glass was still half full and I think he finally realised he'd had enough. I was glad. His speech had become slurred and he was looking blankly as if he was having trouble focusing. But there was still more I wanted to know and there was unlikely to be a better time than this.

"Peter, you said something about understanding more when you got older. What did you mean?"

It was no use. He was starting to sway on his chair and it was as if he could not hear my voice. He did try to speak more, but it was the type of raving you would expect from a drunken man and, as such, made no sense. We left the bar and walked home. He staggered the whole way and I struggled to hold him upright. Grandma was still awake and took him in as if he was a wounded soldier. She got him to bed with all the ease of a well-practiced routine.

Seven

On the twenty-third of the month, just as Rebecca had predicted, Mr Beaufort arrived for a seven-day stay at the hotel. I was alone when I first saw him. He was sitting at the breakfast table, stirring his coffee. He looked older than I expected and I guessed he was in his early to mid-thirties. Despite his age, she had not exaggerated in her description of his attractiveness, which I had wrongly believed of her. He was indeed very handsome. His prominent cheekbones and sturdy jawline gave him a pronounced manliness that almost made him look out of place in a fine hotel. I do not mean the splendour of fine living was above him. Rather that I could easily have pictured him in a more rugged setting, scaling a dangerous mountain or driving an open-top Jeep across a harsh desert, his rifle lying across the seat next to him. He had tough-looking skin that was not of the soft texture one would normally associate with an executive. He was tanned, and his cheeks and neck were darkened even more with rough stubble. It was not the unshaven appearance of an untidy man, or even a man that was hard pressed for time. Rather, it was of a man who took care to do things in his own time, and at his own pace. He continued to stir his coffee in a slow and calculated manner that had the perception of a daily ritual he maintained regardless of where in the world he might be. He looked around the room without pausing or focusing on anyone or anything in particular, yet leaving me with little doubt he had taken in everything in minute detail.

I crossed the breakfast room on an errand to relay a

message to Rodrigo in the kitchen. I purposely passed behind Mr Beaufort, but alerted by a sixth sense or perhaps some other deep-seated instinct, his head turned until his line of vision had captured the intruder. For that was how I felt when his dark blue eyes locked me in their line of sight. I was the thief that was surprised by the detective, I was the rabbit caught in the glare of the car's headlights. At first, I detected disappointment in his glance. Perhaps the blur of my black uniform had made him think it was Rebecca, but faced with a stranger, his expression betrayed him. Yet in the split second our eyes met, he warmed to the stranger, and the corners of his lips arched upwards as a polite smile took hold. Then I was gone, as swiftly as I had appeared, into the warm and noisy din of the kitchen.

It was a fine day considering the lateness of the year. A scattering of pale clouds dotted the blue sky as they drifted aimlessly in from the sea. I felt the sun's warmth on my face, although I could not see it as it was low in the autumn sky and hidden behind the tall city buildings.

Rebecca and I walked to Stephen's Green during our lunch break. It was a great relief to leave the bustling streets behind and lose ourselves in the blissful serenity of the park. We strolled across the smooth lawns that led down to the lake and found an empty bench to sit on. We sat for a while without talking and watched a multitude of ducks paddle furiously as they raced one another to win small pieces of bread. The small white lumps were flung into the water by various groups of schoolchildren. Two magnificent swans swept down from above and gilded majestically across the lake, their white wings outstretched. The two birds resembled silent gliders floating on an unseen breeze. Simultaneously, both birds lowered their webbed feet when only a few feet from the water's surface. With graceful skill, the two giants broke the calm film of water and their bodies settled down into the lake with barely a splash to be seen. Wave after wave of gentle rippling water spread out, making their predetermined journeys in concentric circles to every corner of the lake.

"I met him in the corridor," she said.

"Did he say anything?"

"He smiled and said, 'Good morning, Rebecca.'"

"How did he know your name?"

"From his last visit. He was at the main desk and heard the receptionist call me by name." She sat up straight as she thought about it. "Imagine that, Anna, he remembered my name and then used it to greet me this morning. What do you think about that?" Her face could no longer conceal the excitement that had being building up all morning.

I had wondered why she had not mentioned Mr Beaufort earlier today and I suspected she did not trust me. I had mentioned my doubts before and, as such, my loyalty was in question. But now she had thrown caution to the wind and included me in her euphoria once again. I knew I had to watch what I said, to choose my words with care and tread lightly with her feelings.

"The fact he remembered your name when he could so easily have passed without even a glance does mean something, no doubt about it." I nodded as I spoke, so there would be no mistake I thought it a positive development.

"It was a prelude to asking me out, that's what it was."

I held her hand and said, "Please be careful about this, Rebecca."

Confusion spread across her face before she spoke. "What do you mean?"

"You don't know anything about him. Maybe he was just being polite and that's all there was to it," I said, completely ignoring my own silent advice about treading carefully.

"Oh for heaven's sake, Anna. Why can't you be more positive? That's what I need, not someone to dampen my dreams."

"I'm sorry. Please forgive me, I just don't want to see you get hurt, that's all."

After an awkward moment of silence, she smiled. "Of course I forgive you," she said, squeezing my hand to reinforce her words.

I decided to try and appear positive, for her sake and for the sake of our friendship. I could only hope the niggling doubts in the back of my mind would prove unfounded.

"He might need a *push* to encourage him," I said, and her face brightened at my apparent change of attitude.

"I have it all planned," she said in an excited voice. "I'm

going to clean his room early tomorrow. I'll time it just right and be there when he returns after his breakfast."

I was quiet for a few moments, a little stunned by her plan. Not just the plan, but the conceiving of such an idea. She had it all worked out, calculated, and timed all for one simple purpose—to put Mr Beaufort in a situation where he would see an opportunity to invite her out. Little would he know she would have led him to the moment. If I knew him, I might feel sorry for him, for it would be most embarrassing if his intentions were not as she maintained. But I did not know him. He was a stranger, a man at a breakfast table, a hotel guest, and just another one of the many unknown faces that came and went, day after day.

I arrived home to find Grandpa in a foul mood. He was stomping around the house and finding fault with everyone and everything. Grandma busied herself in the kitchen making sure to keep out of his way. Peter had sought sanctuary in the safety of his room.

I was less fortunate. I went into the parlour to heat myself at the fire, but he walked straight in after me. What I would have given for the ground to open and swallow me up at that moment. As it was, I had nowhere to go. To leave the room after having just entered would be embarrassing, not to mention blatantly obvious. I smiled as best I could in recognition of his presence. He tried to return my smile, but what appeared on his cold face was more similar to a sneer, which he followed with a pig-like grunt.

"How is the job going?" he asked, but his voice was mocking, as if I had no business working.

"Fine," I said.

That was the extent of our conversation. We sat in silence listening to the crackling of burning turf and the low roar of flames shooting up the chimney. Neither of us knew what to say to the other and I don't think either of us wanted to say anything. I waited for ten agonising minutes to pass before I felt it all right to stand and leave the room.

"Goodnight," I said.

He did not reply.

Eight

We stood waiting on the footpath, two buildings away from the hotel. The sky was a cold blue, but nevertheless a glorious sapphire colour. It was the type that helped to lift one's spirit should it need a boost. We were cold, excited, and apprehensive all at the same time. A gentle but chilly November breeze blew through the streets of Dublin and chilled the Saturday morning shoppers that hurried by, bags in hand, their heads covered with woolly and peaked caps alike.

There were many times in my life when I felt awkward, like I did not belong, or like a fish out of water. This was one of those times.

Rebecca continuously twisted and stretched her neck around to look out for Mr Beaufort's rented car. I looked too, but more with minor dread than with the excited aspirations she was experiencing. She had not told him I would be accompanying them on their outing. What would he think? Would he be angry? Disappointed? Confused? Whatever his reaction, I'd be the one left to feel the embarrassment, certainly not Rebecca. No, it was me that would be the odd one out.

At midday, the precise moment the two hands on my watch touched twelve, a large grey car pulled in against the kerb. The driver honked the horn, and there he was, leaning over to peer out the passenger window.

"This is my friend, Anna," Rebecca said as she slid across the back seat.

"Anna," he said with delight in his voice. "It's a great

pleasure to meet you."

"And you," I said, as polite and ladylike as was possible for me.

It was the first time I had heard my name pronounced with a French accent, and I had to admit, it sent a warm tingle jingling through my body.

His smile, his manner, and his handshake all had the effect of instantly putting me at ease. It was as if at the mere click of a finger, my anxieties vanished as rapidly as air escapes from an exploding balloon.

"You must give me directions, mademoiselles" —*there went that tingle again*— "I do not know where this Howth village is."

I did not know either, but Rebecca did, and guided him through the busy city streets and onto the coast road.

"Straight all the way now," she said, pointing the way. "It's about a twenty minute drive."

He drove carefully. I expect it was strange for him to be driving on the wrong side of the road, or was it the right side? I could never understand why they drove on the opposite side of the road on the continent.

"My nan told me all about Howth," I said to the both of them, desperately trying not to appear embarrassed.

"You have never been to this lovely Howth Rebecca told me about?" he asked, his dark eyes glancing at me in the rear-view mirror.

"No," I said, and went on to explain how I recently moved to the city, but without mentioning the death of my mother.

I caught a sudden glare from Rebecca in the corner of my eye. It wasn't anger, but it wasn't encouragement either. I was doing too much talking. This was her date and I was only along for the ride. I went quiet as I knew she wanted, and just hoped Mr Beaufort would say something to her next.

He did. "Rebecca, tell me about this Howth village, please."

"Oh, it's lovely," she said, leaning forward to talk to him. "You can walk out along the harbour and eat ice cream as you go!"

I was dying to speak, which was quite unlike me, but I didn't. I remained silent while they talked, and I gazed out at the incoming tide washing up along the pebbled coastline.

"Please, call me, Pierre," he said at one point. "Mr Beaufort sounds so formal, and we are friends, are we not?"

"Pierre," Rebecca said, obviously pleased at being able to use his Christian name. She didn't just say it once, she repeated it again, slowly the second time, so the named rolled off her tongue with a poetic sound.

As Rebecca had said, Howth was not far from the city, barely a twenty minute drive along the coast road. We rounded a bend and the harbour opened up before us. It was divided into two sections by a long sea wall, one side for the fishing fleet and the other for privately owned sailing boats. The fishing fleet was in and trawlers of every size and colour were tied to the wharf by thick ropes that sagged under their own weight and dipped low just above the water's surface. The sky was dotted with hundreds of birds, mostly gulls as they hovered in circles and swooped down when they spotted a tasty morsel of fish that was thrown aside by one of the fishermen. We drove along the harbour road, with the boats on one side, and a multitude of restaurants, bars, fish-and-chip shops, and ice cream parlours on the other. Pierre parked the car and the three of us got out with all the excitement of children visiting the beach.

"This is beautiful," Pierre said as his glance alternated between the multi-coloured trawlers and the Hill of Howth that dominated the village, its slopes bathed in rich green foliage.

"Will we walk to the end of the pier?" I asked.

"Yes." They answered simultaneously.

"That will be nice," Pierre added.

And so we walked. Rebecca and I linked arms and huddled to ward off the bitter breeze blowing in from the sea. Pierre walked alongside us, carefully choosing Rebecca's side, I noticed.

It was a long walk along the stone wall that stretched out and around to the mouth of the harbour. We stepped carefully around fishing nets that were laid out along the path as they underwent repairs.

"Look," Pierre said while pointing past the trawlers.

Seals were poking their heads above the surface, and one of the boat's crew, seeing them, emptied a bucket of fish heads and guts over the side of his boat. The seals disappeared again beneath the surface in search of their sinking meal.

"Are you from Paris?" Rebecca asked him.

"No, I'm from the Bordeaux region."

"Is that where they make wine?" I asked.

"Yes," he said, his face lighting up. "Bordeaux is the home of many vineyards. In the summer, the sweet scent from the vines envelopes the countryside, and it is really very, very beautiful."

"It sounds lovely," I said.

"It is. When I was a child, we would help crush the grapes using our bare feet. We'd stomp and stomp until our legs and feet turned red from the grape juice."

I smiled at the thought of him, a small child wearing short trousers and crushing the grapes with his bare feet.

"But now," he said, with a look of sadness in his eyes. "It is all done by machine, not like the old days."

"Do you visit Paris often?" Rebecca asked.

"No, not often," he said, a glint of boredom in his face, but she did not notice. It was obvious to me anyway, that he would rather talk about Bordeaux, and its rolling hills carpeted in forests of vines, than the metropolis of Paris.

We stood at the end of the harbour wall and looked out to sea. Two teenage boys sat on the edge, their legs dangling free over the side. They held fishing poles, the lines stretched taut and down into the grey swirling water below them.

"I'm frozen, let's go back," Rebecca said.

I shrugged. I was likewise frozen, but there was something invigorating about standing there. The smell of the sea, the salt-laden wind filtering through my hair, the sight of the ocean tumbling towards us as white crested wave after wave rolled forward, like some medieval army charging in formation to their doom. I saw the same captivating feeling in Pierre's eyes. He was struck by the sheer awe of the scene. The wonder of the ocean was holding us there, gripping us in the moment.

"Well, come on," Rebecca said, her back already turned in her eagerness to escape the magnificence of nature for a bland ice cream parlour, or some greasy spoon cafe.

Pierre turned to follow. His eyes caught mine for the briefest of moments. There was resignation in his look, I could tell. He would have stayed in that spot for as long as he could have braved the cold, as would I.

Pierre insisted on buying us lunch. We picked a nice-looking restaurant that also had tables and chairs outside, but it was much too cold to sit in the open air. We chose a window that had a panoramic view of the bay. I sat facing him while Rebecca opted for the chair beside our host. It was a great treat and I studied the menu, my mouth watering at the selection of luscious desserts.

To my surprise, I was enjoying the day so far. Rebecca's Frenchman was polite and pleasant, and a good deal quieter than I had expected. He told us about his job and answered all our questions about France. Despite being the gooseberry, his general demeanour made me feel not the slightest bit uncomfortable. When we finished eating, he ordered drinks for us all. I asked for a mineral while they both had a glass of beer.

"Mademoiselles," Pierre said while lifting his glass. "I wish to thank you for a most pleasant day. Santé!"

We raised our glasses and accompanied the toast with giggles, much to his amusement.

"When do you have to leave?" Rebecca asked him.

"Monday, I'm flying to London," he replied.

"We'll miss you," she said, and reached out to place her hand on his.

"Will you?" he said, and turned his hand over, enclosing his fingers around hers.

I looked out the window, not wanting to intrude on their moment. The room was warm and it felt odd looking out into the cold of the day. A single pane of thin glass separated the cosiness of the restaurant from the blustery scene outside. Little had changed since we came inside. Birds flocked around the fishing boats, hoping to pick up discarded scraps, and the grey sea continued its unrelenting roll toward land.

An elderly couple bundled up in heavy coats and scarfs walked the harbour wall as we had done. He linked her arm and there was something comforting about the bond of the distant pair. I imagined they had been married for forty...no, fifty years. Perhaps they had been childhood sweethearts. Their children were grown up now and had families of their own. Now they had time on their hands, time for each another, even after all those years. In the day, they'd walk, taking in the sights—familiar sights they'd seen a hundred times before. In the evening, they'd sit close to the fire, drinking coco and reminiscing as the flames flickered and danced before them. Someday, I thought with sadness, one of them would succumb to old age and pass away. It would not be long before the other, lost and broken-hearted, followed their beloved partner to the afterlife. They'd lie together in some windswept cemetery, and once in a while, a fresh bunch of flowers would appear when one of their children found the time.

"Anna?" Rebecca's voice broke into my thoughts.

"Yes...sorry, what did you say?" I realised from the mystified look on her face she had been talking to me.

"I said we are going back into town. Maybe we'll go to the cinema."

"Will you come to the cinema?" Pierre asked, sounding genuinely inviting.

"No, I'll go home. You two go and enjoy yourselves."

"Are you sure—"

Rebecca interrupted Pierre. "No, she's fine. Your gran wanted you home early, didn't she, Anna?"

"Yes, that's right, she did," I said, reinforcing her lie.

"That is a shame. Maybe next time," Pierre said.

"Yes, maybe next time."

The drive back into the city did not take long, seemingly shorter than the trip out. It was probably because it lacked the unknown expectations of what was to come, and the excitement was gone. Rebecca sat up front this time next to Pierre. Every now and again, her hand would reach out to touch his as they spoke. Now I felt awkward, the gooseberry, the unwanted friend.

They dropped me off at the end of my road. Pierre was quick to jump out and open my door for me. Very gentlemanly, I thought. I froze with embarrassment when he kissed me on one cheek and then the other. Then they were gone. The grey outline of the car blended into the moving traffic, leaving me alone on the corner of Dorset Street and Ignatius Road.

Nine

The house was cold. Grandpa had said we could not afford to light the fire during the day because the price of coal had gone up again. That was all right for him, I thought. *He always goes out in the afternoons, but poor Grandma and I have to sit shivering while looking into an empty fireplace.*

Grandma made some tea and brought in two cups, a milk jug, and a tea pot. They were neatly laid out on a tray that had a painting of a quaint country cottage reproduced across its surface. The teapot was hidden in a hand-knitted tea cosy. I told her about my morning, describing the scenery of Howth in detail. She had been there before, but my vivid descriptions of the fishing fleet and the white crested waves breaking over the rocks seemed to fill her heart with joy and happy memories.

"It's been so long since I was there," she said. "When we were courting, your grandpa and I would jump on a tram and ride it all the way to the last stop in Howth."

"There are no trams now, only buses," I said.

"I know," she replied mournfully. "It's a shame. The trams were wonderful, rocking along on their rails, the driver ringing the bell if anyone stepped in front of him."

"We should go someday, just you and me," I said.

"Oh, that would be wonderful!" She smiled and her tired old eyes widened in delight.

"Did you ever go anywhere with my mother?" I asked, and added, "Just the two of you, I mean."

Her face grew sad again as her thoughts turned to her

daughter. "When Maria was young, I'd push her buggy all the way to the Phoenix Park. I'd buy ice cream and we'd sit on the steps of the monument watching the boys play football and families having picnics." Her smile returned with the memory.

"And when she was older?" I asked.

"Not so much then. Maria had lots of friends and we hardly ever saw her."

"Gran?" I said in a low voice.

"Yes?"

"Why did she leave?"

"Oh that's all so long ago, it doesn't matter much now," she said with a hint of panic in her eyes.

I watched as she became uneasy in her seat, shifting around.

"Gran," I said, reaching out to place my hand on hers. "I know you don't want to talk about it, but don't you think it's unfair to leave me wondering?"

She settled back into the chair, her uneasiness receding as she turned her hand face-up to hold mine.

"You are right, child, you do have a right to know. I will tell you, but not just yet. I need time to strengthen myself before talking about it. You see, the day Maria left was the last day I saw my beloved child. It was the day I lost her, lost my baby. I just need some time before I talk about it, you understand, don't you?"

"Of course I do." I slid forward from my chair and knelt beside her, wrapping my arms around her thin shoulders.

She rested her head against my chest and sobbed quietly. I said nothing else and left conversation at that.

The rain returned on Monday morning, but did little to dampen the smile on Rebecca's face when I called for her. We walked fast, as people tend to do in the rain, and huddled together under an umbrella. She was fit to explode with happiness as she related everything there was to know about the time she and Pierre spent together after leaving me. *Pierre said this... Pierre said that... We went here... We went there.* I listened as friends do, allowing myself to be a sponge that absorbed her overflowing excitement.

From what she told me, Pierre sounded completely genuine, and it seemed any doubts I had about him were unfounded. She had met with him again on Sunday and spent the day walking around the city. They had strolled hand-in-hand along the banks of the Grand Canal and sat on one of the benches that were along its route. It was quiet, she said, and sheltered by the branches of an overhanging willow tree. They listened to the water trickling through one of the lock gates. He kissed her, she told me. Not an awkward teenage kiss with noses bumping and tongues flapping wildly, but a long, slow, sensual kiss filled with tenderness and meaning.

"He'll be back next Saturday," she said. "He had to catch an early flight to London this morning."

"I thought he only came to Dublin every four or five weeks?" I said.

"Normally, yes, but his company is trying to finalise some big contract, so he will be here a lot over the next eight weeks."

"That's good, isn't it?" I said.

"It's wonderful! Eight weeks is all I need," she said, her voice brimming with excitement.

"Need for what?" I asked.

"To get him to propose, of course," she said, smiling in mischief as we pushed our way through the hotel's revolving doors.

It was dinner time before we had a chance to talk again. We sat in the corner of the kitchen as Rodrigo gave us each a plate of steaming hot lasagne.

"Eat, girls, eat!" he encouraged us with his usual hearty laugh and almost impossible to understand English.

From the first day I met Rodrigo, I decided I liked him. He was a big man with a big stomach that seemed apt considering his occupation. I often watched him struggle down the kitchen aisle, using one hand to manoeuvre his sagging belly around obstacles. What really endeared me to him was his happy-go-lucky personality that was practically infectious. I don't believe I ever once saw any of the kitchen staff looking stressed or down, regardless of what pressure they might be under in the busy kitchen. The cheery atmosphere could undoubtedly be traced back to one man, Rodrigo, the head chef.

Rodrigo returned to check on the ovens and I turned to

Rebecca. "Rebecca, are you sure getting married is what you want? I mean, you've only known this guy for five minutes."

"Are you kidding?" she said with a look of astonishment. "He's good-looking, he's not poor...and he's my ticket out of here."

"I know, but—"

"But what?"

"But, it just seems all a bit too good to be true, that's all."

"Oh for heaven's sake, Anna, why do you always think the worst? Always negative. Why can't you just be happy for me, and maybe just a bit more supportive?"

"I am happy for you. It's just—"

"Just what?"

"It's just that maybe he's not thinking about marriage. It's an awful big thing you know...getting married."

"Don't you worry, he wants to marry me. Maybe he doesn't realise it yet, but he will." She grinned with a deviant smile that was full of self-assurance. "He just needs a little persuasion, that's all."

The steady drum of music from Peter's room penetrated the thin wall between us without respite, but the music was not what was on my mind as I stood motionless at the side of my bed. I was looking at my suitcase. It was sitting on the end of the bed and not underneath where I had left it this morning. I knew I was not mistaken. I always left it under the bed, only taking it out when I wanted something. The zip was only pulled halfway around. The perpetrator had not even bothered to hide the evidence of their rummaging.

I knocked on Peter's door.

"Yeah?" he answered.

"It's me, can I come in?"

"Of course."

I pushed the door open. The room was a haze of smoke. A cigarette was sitting in an ashtray on the window sill. The window was slightly ajar, but the wind was blowing the smoke back into the room. Peter was sitting on the bed, a pillow propped up between him and the wall. He reached out to turn down the volume on the radio that was on the bed-side locker.

"What's wrong, little niece?"

"Have you been in my room?" I asked. I was polite and not accusing, convinced there would be a simple explanation for my case having been opened.

"No," he said, shaking his head slowly from side to side. "Why do you ask?"

"Someone has looked through my case and I was wondering why."

"Ah," he said as if realising something. "That would have been Dad. I thought I heard him going in there earlier."

"But why would he want to go through my things?" I asked.

"I don't know. That's something you'll have to ask him."

I returned to my room, confused and upset at the thought of him going through my belongings. I decided to ask him about it. Perhaps there was an innocent explanation, but I was at a loss as to what that reason could be.

My grandparents were sitting in the parlour. The fire was lit and the flames from the burning coal basked the walls in a warm orange glow. They were not talking. Grandma was knitting and he sat close to the fireplace, half dozing, but definitely awake. I sat down to face him. My stomach felt as if there were butterflies flittering around it and my mouth had suddenly gone dry.

"Grandpa," I said.

"Yes?" His head rose, his face looking drowsy as his eyes tried to focus on me.

"Was there something you wanted in my room?" I asked.

His expression hardened. I kept facing him, but in the corner of my eye, I noticed Grandma stop what she was doing and remain perfectly still as if she had turned into a statue.

"Why do you ask that?" he growled.

I was terrified, but I'd come this far. "My case was out and Peter thought you had been in there."

"And what of it?" His voice was dismissive.

I looked to Grandma for help, but she said nothing, looking as scared as I felt.

"But why would you have to go through my case?" I finally said.

He stared at me coldly for a few moments before speaking. It was as if he held my question and even my nerve for asking it in contempt. "When you live under our roof" —I believe he meant *his roof*— "we are responsible for your wellbeing. You are a young girl and this is a big city. A naive country lassie can easily go astray here."

"But I'm not a child. I'm eighteen next week. I don't understand. Anyway, what has rummaging through my belongings got to do with it?"

His face grew red and his fingers dug into the side of the chair. I could tell he was on the point of exploding but was trying his utmost to hold it in. I didn't care. I was angry, even if it did not show.

"We need to know where you are and who you're with. Like I said, you are our responsibility."

"I go to work every day and then come back here. What else is there to know?" I asked as defiantly as I could without raising my voice. As I waited for him to reply, I could not help feeling somewhat pathetic for pointing out my poor social life.

"And what about last Saturday?" he said smugly, as if he knew something I didn't.

"Saturday?"

"That's right, Saturday. Don't think you were invisible. I saw you." His voice was condescending.

"I went to Howth with Rebecca and Pierre. Gran knows that."

"I told him that." Grandma's feeble voice came from behind me.

"And who is this Pierre?" Grandpa asked.

"He's Rebecca's boyfriend. What does it matter anyway?"

"It matters..." He paused for a moment, as if trying to summon up more venom in his voice. "It matters when he has his hands all over you in the middle of the street for all to see."

"What?" I blurted out in disbelief.

"I saw you, letting him slobber all over you, like...like a common tart."

I was speechless, unable to form a reply in my head, let alone actually give one.

"Disgusting," he added.

I finally composed myself. "He gave me a kiss on the cheek. That's what people do, you know."

"Huh!" He grunted.

There was so much I wanted to say. *What I do is my business. And even if he was kissing me, so what? What has it got to do with you?* But I said nothing more. What was the point? How could I reason with someone like that?

I went upstairs and sat on my bed. His smug, self-righteous look remained fixed in my mind, and I found it hard to shrug the image. I suspected I was beginning to know how my mother felt when she lived here and possibly why she left. His overpowering desire for control over the family was suffocating. Knowing my mother as I did, it would not surprise me to find out she simply packed her bag one day and walked out the door, perhaps telling him what she thought of him before she left. At that moment, that's exactly what I felt like doing. But where could I go? I didn't have enough money to rent a room, and imposing myself on Rebecca in her already cramped flat might wreck my friendship with her.

I decided to save my money and, as soon as I had a deposit for a room, I would move out. The thought of leaving made me feel happy and washed away some of the hurt I felt.

Ten

Rebecca confided in me less and less as the weeks slipped past. Pierre was in Dublin more often than not, and any spare time he had was spent in her company. Their relationship was obviously going well. I would see their faces light up whenever they caught sight of each another in the hotel. They never stopped to talk—at least I never saw them do so. But they never failed to acknowledge the other's presence with a look that could only be conveyed by lovers. It was as if a secret affair was in motion and should the lovers be discovered, she would be deemed guilty of breaking some unwritten hotel rule that prohibited the fraternisation between guests and staff. If there was such a rule, unwritten or otherwise, I had not heard of it, but I imagine the hotel's management would not have looked favourably on Rebecca's liaisons with one of the guests.

I suspect my raising concerns about him had resulted in her deciding not to include me with the ins and outs of their romance. I fell in with her wishes and did not bring up the subject. She was still pleasant to me and we still walked to work together, talking and joking as friends do. But something was missing. A line had been drawn and I was not to cross it. The result was, while still friends, an invisible rift had opened up between us, and our friendship had suffered. There was little I could do, other than respect her wishes and be there should she need me.

—◦◦◦◦◦—

The second of December was my birthday. I was eighteen years old and an adult in the eyes of the law, but not in the eyes of Grandpa. His oppressive nature continued to get worse. He had begun to question me on a daily basis about my movements and whom I associated with.

Grandma gave me a card with a ten pound note inside. I noticed the card was signed, *Birthday wishes from Grandma and Peter*. There was no mention of Grandpa's name and, despite Grandma hugging me, he sat stony-faced at the kitchen table, doggedly refusing to acknowledge my big day. In a way, I was glad. I would have found it uncomfortable to thank him for anything, even for wishing me a happy birthday.

It was Saturday morning and I asked Grandma if she would like to go out somewhere. Her face brightened with the expectation of a child being given a treat.

"Where will we go?" she asked.

"I have an idea," I said. "But it's a surprise."

"What about dinner?" Grandpa said, his eyes staring hard at her in an effort to remind her of her responsibilities.

"You and Peter will have to look after yourselves today. Anna and I are going out." She spoke as she disappeared out into the hall and her voice was replaced by the soft patter of her slippers on the staircase.

His eyes narrowed and, while he did not say another word, the look of disgust was self-evident. I turned to leave the room, holding in a smile until my back was to him. As I left the kitchen, I was grinning like the Cheshire cat. I'm not sure which pleased me more, the fact we were going out, or Grandma's stance.

Several buses passed as we stood at the bus shelter. I watched her look of confusion as I let each one go by. All the buses went through the city centre before crossing to the south side of Dublin, so it was a mystery to her why we were not getting on any of them. Eventually, I stepped forward and held out my arm as a number forty-two approached. The double-decker bus pulled in. We got on and found a seat.

"Wherever are we going?" she asked, delighted with the intrigue and probably hoping I would not spoil it by divulging our destination.

"You'll see. Be patient, Gran," I said, patting her arm.

The bus winded its way through the narrow streets of the inner city as it drove toward the river. We talked little as we watched the old and grey bricked buildings pass our window like one of those fake scenery reels that revolved around and around, showing similar building after building. The conductor came down and took our fares. He was full of witty chat, and Grandma surprised me with her quick and equally witty replies. A jovial banter followed and the two of them spilled out clever remarks with ease. I remained quiet throughout the verbal exchange, too slow minded to join in with the fast flowing conversation. *It's a Dublin thing,* I thought. The conductor continued on toward the back of the bus and, without pausing to take a breath, continued his flow of clever repartee with another woman.

We crossed Capel Street Bridge and swung right, travelling along the south quays. On one side, the dark green water of the Liffey flowed quickly toward the city centre before it spilled out into Dublin Bay. The sprawling warehouses of the Guinness plant dominated the view on the opposite side as the bus picked up speed. It was only when we turned right and crossed back over to the north side that she finally put two and two together.

"The park," she exclaimed, proud to have solved the mystery.

"Yes," I said, smiling. "I thought it would be nice. I've still not seen it."

"Oh, Anna," she said, a tear welling up in the corner of her eye. "You remembered me telling you how I brought Maria there. How thoughtful of you, child."

"We can get ice cream and watch the boys playing football," I said.

"Oh, Anna, I'm so happy." She reached out to squeeze my hand with her frail grip.

We got off opposite the main gates. Huge stone pillars marked the park's entrance and a constant stream of traffic swung in through the wide openings as if fleeing the city en masse. We crossed the road and walked through, entering a more beautiful domain as we did. We left the drab and grey buildings with all their depressing uniformity behind and found ourselves faced with a world dominated by green.

The main road stretched into the distance as far as the eye could see, with grassy fields lining both sides. Two wide footpaths separated the road from the verdant meadows and every fifty feet or so, old gas lamps sat perched on shiny black poles that resembled regimental soldiers marching in single file. Beyond the leas, forests surrounded the park and, for a brief moment, I felt I was on a rural walk back in County Sligo.

We strolled slowly, arm-in-arm, breathing in the fresh air and absorbing the peaceful scene. The trees to our left petered out and the impressive Wellington monument came into view. The grey stone obelisk rose defiantly into the clear blue sky, the steep surrounding steps reminding me of pictures I'd seen of Egypt's pyramids. Bronze plaques surrounded the base of the column, and Grandma told me they were cast from French cannons captured at the Battle of Waterloo.

The monument was a hundred yards in from the road and the scene seemed uncannily unchanged from her descriptions of visits some forty years ago. Groups of lads were kicking footballs, their jumpers on the ground marking the goalposts for which they eagerly strived to place the ball. Couples rambled together, holding hands as if the park's soothing ambiance was drawing their bond closer. Under the watchful eyes of parents, children ran and played in the never-ending grassy expanse of the park.

An ice cream van was parked along the road, nestled between parked cars. We asked for two 99s—cones with a large dollop of rich cream and a chocolate flake protruding up from the centre. Grandma fumbled in her purse for change, but I was quick to produce the correct money, keen to ensure the day was my treat.

We walked across the field to the bottom steps of the monument. We manoeuvred our cones at various angles to compensate for the melting cream that was beginning to trickle down the sides. We struck up the steps like mountaineers attacking a mountain. Leaning forward to cope with the sharp incline, we made our way up to the top step where we sat to enjoy the view below us.

As I sat next to her, neither of us talked, both absorbed in the pleasurable preoccupation of eating our cones. I had one of those deja vu moments were I felt I had been there before, in that exact spot. But of course that was impossible. However, my mother had been there, sitting with Grandma just as I was, many years ago and long before I was born. At that moment, my mind became awash with mixed feelings of sadness mingled with happiness. I missed my mother. I missed the words she used to soothe me when I was down. I missed her soft, reassuring voice that lifted my spirit when it waned. I missed her sweet smell, a smell that enraptured love and safety for me. But my heart felt something else also. It was the feeling I was experiencing a special moment— a moment that would carry with me for the rest of my life. It would be a memory that someday, God willing, I might share with a child of my own. I pictured myself telling them how I once sat here with their great-grandmother, and how the scene remained unchanged in all those years.

After a while, we descended the sloping steps of the monument and walked farther into the park, leaving the stone structure and the boys kicking footballs behind us. Trails led away from the road and weaved their way in a crisscross fashion through the many forests. We breathed in the stillness of the woods where the intenseness of the solitude was only disturbed by small animals going about their daily activities, seemingly unafraid or simply oblivious of our presence.

"You never met my father, did you, Grandma?" I asked as we walked.

She paused before answering, almost embarrassed at my question for some reason. "No...why do you ask?"

"Oh, I don't know. He died when I was so young, it would be nice to hear someone talk about him."

"Didn't Maria tell you about him?" she asked.

"Yes, Mother told me how they met after she left Dublin. She never talked about the accident. It made her sad to recall the night it happened."

"Oh you poor thing," she said, linking my arm. "I don't know much, except it was a car crash while he was returning home late one night."

"I could never understand—"

"Understand what?" she interrupted.

"Why she did not tell me more about him. The type of man he was, the things he would say, and how...how much he loved me."

There was silence for a few moments. I was feeling emotional, and I think she felt unsure about how to console me.

"I'm sure he must have loved you, Anna," she said,

squeezing my hand.

"But that's just it," I said.

"What do you mean?" she asked.

"That's what I feel, I'm sure he *must* have loved me. I should *know* he loved me. Why don't I know that for certain without having to think about it?"

"Oh, Anna, he must have loved both you and Maria, I'm sure of that."

"But how can you be sure? You never met him," I said.

"I just know. I don't know how to put it into words for you to understand, but Maria would not have married him if he did not love the both of you."

I stopped. My mind froze for a moment as if a spanner had been tossed into the turning cogs of my mind. *If he had not loved the both of us?*

I turned to look at her. There was a look of horror on her face. She realised she had said something she did not mean to. She bit her lip with nervousness and tried to speak, but could not find the right words to backtrack on what she had said.

"Grandma, why would you say that? If he had not loved *the both* of us?"

"Oh no...I mean...that's not—"

"Grandma, please tell me what you meant," I said as she struggled to speak.

She took a long, deep breath and looked me straight in the eye. I felt her grasp tighten around my hand.

"Oh, Anna, I'm so sorry, I did not mean to upset you. It's just that...well, I suppose you do have a right to know."

"To know what?"

"About your father," she said, calmness having returned to her voice.

"Tell me, Grandma, please tell me the truth."

"I will, my child. Let's go somewhere and sit down. My legs are tired."

We left the park and walked along the shop fronts, looking for a cafe. My stomach was in knots and the anticipation of hearing what she was going to tell me left me feeling weak and a little sick.

Eleven

There were times in the past I remember reading about people, whom upon discovering a momentous truth or untruth about their parents, found themselves lost and questioning their very existence. We all have an identity. It's a simple word that denotes our individuality among others. It encompasses the logical facts about a person—name, address, occupation. It also includes the other factors that set us aside from the billions of other beings on this planet. Our attitude, our beliefs, the way we carry ourselves, and even our unheard inner thoughts all combine to make us who we are. Whilst two people may share the same name, and sometimes even the same address—a father and son, for example—no two people share the same psychological identity. A bit like fingerprints, I suppose.

I'd always felt a comfort within myself, knowing my own identity that is—my thoughts and perception of who I was in the grand scheme of things. But the very stone on which my personal identity was founded was about to be rocked. No, rocked is not the right word. It was about to be kicked out from beneath me. It was to leave me feeling as if my life was a lie and I was a fraud.

We ordered tea in a small snack bar facing Heuston Train Station. It was one of those cafes I'd refer to as a *greasy spoon place.* The tables were small and bunched together. It was hard to tell which chair belonged to which table. The chequered table cloths were those plastic vinyl ones with thick, folded edges that rubbed annoyingly against one's legs. I sat at the window while Grandma paid a visit to the ladies room. I watched various people lugging heavy suitcases as they made their way in and out of the station house. It brought back a brief memory of the night I arrived in Dublin, alone and unsure of what was to become of me. But the memory vanished as quickly as it had appeared, as my mind returned to the look on Grandma's face when she let slip something she had not meant to.

She returned and we sat in silence for a while, watching the people pass by. Neither of us seemed to know how to begin the conversation.

Eventually, I broke the ice. "What did you mean when you said what you did?"

"Anna, I'm so sorry. I was going to tell you someday. It's just that I wanted to wait for the right time."

"The right time?" I asked.

"I can see now there will never be a right time, there would always be some reason to convince me to put it off."

"Put what off? Please, Grandma, please tell me. I think I have a right to know."

"You do, Anna, and now that you are eighteen, I suppose this is as good a time as any to tell you about your father."

"I thought you did not know him?"

"I did not know Maria's husband, but I did know your father."

Her words hit me like a baseball bat. I gasped as I leaned back in my seat, unable to speak. There was sorrow in her eyes as she looked at me, and she took a deep breath before continuing.

"My precious Maria was just seventeen. I knew there was something wrong weeks before she told me. Mothers know things, you know, about their children. From when they are babies, we are aware of the slightest change in their moods. When a baby is unwell, even if there are no symptoms, a mother will know, even if the doctor can find nothing."

"She was pregnant, wasn't she, Grandma?"

She looked at me for a moment, her eyes displaying an intense sadness. It was me sitting before her, but she could not see me. She was looking at Maria, her precious lost child.

"Yes, Anna, she was pregnant," she said, seriousness mingled with the look of despair on her face. "She told me one night when we were alone in the house. It was late and we were sitting at the fire. Maria's cheeks glowed red from the heat, and in her eyes, I saw the flames dancing, as if their reflection was trying to help hide her fears from the outside world."

"What did you do, Grandma?"

"Do?" She leaned forward a little and warmed her hands around the cup. "I did what all mothers would do. I cradled her in my arms while she sobbed like a small child—and she was a small child. She was my baby."

The cloak of silence returned and we sipped our tea. It was a heavy silence, weighed down with the bittersweet memories of a grieving mother. She was hurting inside and I felt her sadness. I missed my mother just as she missed her daughter, and we were united with the pain.

I asked the woman behind the counter for another pot of tea, and Grandma waited until she left our table before speaking again.

"It was all so long ago, but it still feels like yesterday—and it always will be only yesterday, in my heart."

"Who was my father?" I asked, feeling guilty for asking, as if it was a forbidden question.

"I thought"—she straightened herself up as she summoned all her inner strength—"it would be some boy she met at a dance, but I was wrong. He was a teacher at her school."

"A teacher?" I said, a horrifying expression spreading across my face.

"Yes, Anna, a teacher. His name was Robert Cleary. He was her English teacher. I should say he took advantage of her, and he did, I suppose, but in a way, I can understand."

How can she understand? I thought, thinking back to my own school and our English teacher, Mr Wilson, a balding middle-aged and overweight man that always wore a moth-eaten jacket. I felt physical ill for a moment.

She spoke again, interrupting the vile image in my mind. "You see, Robert Cleary was not much older than her. He was twenty and, having finished his training, it was his first teaching job. And Maria, well I know I said she was my baby and that was true, for she would always be my baby, but she was a grown woman. She looked older than she was, and she was mature for her age, too mature for boys the same age as her. They bored her with their immaturity. And to be honest, they looked like small children when they were with her."

"You sound like you almost condone what happened," I said, trying to keep any hint of an accusing tone out of my voice.

"Oh no, Anna, please don't misunderstand me. It was terrible and, at the time, I was angry, shocked, and I wanted to storm down to the school and shout blue murder from its roof."

"But you didn't?"

"No, I'm ashamed to say I did not."

"Why?" I asked.

She did not answer, and looked down, sadness in her eyes, probably wishing she could rewind time to handle the situation differently.

"Why not, Grandma?"

"Because of your grandfather. It was later on, after we told him. He said he did not want the world knowing our business."

"So you never made a complaint?"

"No, Anna, I didn't. Patrick said he would handle it and I was to keep out of it."

We left the cafe. We had finished our tea and felt uncomfortable by the woman's continuous glances toward our table, waiting for us to order more or leave. So leave we did and walked the short distance to the War Memorial Gardens. The gardens were beautiful and the smell from tended flower beds filled the air with a sweet aroma. We sat on a bench near the wall of names. Row after row of engraved letters covered the black-marbled surface, each one a name, once a living soul that walked and talked, and existed. Now their names were just a reminder, a reminder of a futile war that decimated a generation.

There was a calm blanket of peacefulness that hung over the park. The surrounding trees dampened the noise of passing traffic until the rumble of cars was no louder than the gentle wind that drifted carelessly across the green lawns.

"Is that why my mother left, because she was pregnant?" I finally said, breaking the silence.

"Not quite, that was only part of it."

"How do you mean?"

"Patrick did not take the news very well."

"Was he angry?" As I asked the question, I pictured his

cold expression of contempt any time he looked at me. He was not the sort of man I would want to break such news to.

"Yes, Anna, he was furious. There were terrible rows after we told him. Oh he said such wicked things to her, things I could never repeat." She pulled a handkerchief from her bag and sobbed into it.

I put my arm around her shoulders and tried to console her.

"That's why she left." She wiped the tears from her eyes, struggling to control her emotions. "Maria packed a suitcase and said she was leaving. I begged her to stay, but he told her to get out and never to come back."

"So she left?"

"Yes, she kissed me goodbye and walked out the door. That was the last time I saw my darling child. She wrote soon after and told me where she was staying, but he forbade me from contacting her."

"He forbade you?"

"Yes. You must understand, Anna, they were different times then. A wife was expected to obey her husband. And that's what I did. I'll never forgive him for what he did, and I can never forgive myself for listening to him."

I remained quiet for a while as I absorbed all she had told me. Then my thoughts turned to this teacher, this Robert Cleary.

"What about Robert Cleary?"

"I don't know much about what happened to him. As I said, I wanted to go to the school and complain, but your grandfather refused. He said Maria was to blame for flaunting herself and the fault was with her alone. He also said she had brought shame to the family name."

"But, he was her teacher," I said in disbelief. "Surely it was obvious he had acted inappropriately?"

"To you, Anna, yes. To me as well, but not your grandfather. To him, she was solely to blame. 'A loose woman,' he called her."

"So nothing happened to him?" I said in disbelief.

"No," she replied. "But there must have been rumours in the school, because a few weeks later, he was transferred. I don't know to where."

Silence returned again as we sat together on the wooden bench. I held her hand and felt her weak fingers grasp mine as tightly as they could. Around us, birds flew from tree to tree, and a squirrel appeared and disappeared, only to show himself again soon after. The wonder of nature continued as it always had, unaware and unable to pause for the grief of any one living thing, regardless of their pain.

There wasn't much talk on the way home. We walked along the quays and caught a bus near Capel Street. The bus was packed with shoppers, all eager to return home with their bags. Grandma sat looking out the window while I stood holding onto the rail that ran along the ceiling. The journey seemed to take forever. My mind was a maelstrom of emotions and questions. The heat was unbearable with people packed like sardines into the bus. Every time the doors opened to let passengers on or off, a welcome blast of cold air would come rushing toward me. That blast of fresh air was the only thing that got me through the journey. Otherwise, the overwhelming feelings of claustrophobia would have forced me to get off, leaving Grandma to finish the journey alone.

$\mathcal{T}$welve

The following days passed in something of a daze. Looking back, I can't seem to remember anything specific about what I did or where I went. If I did try to recall, it was like trying to remember the details of a hazy dream, shrouded in confusion and lacking visual clarity.

I walked to and from the hotel on my own. Rebecca had taken some holiday time from work while Pierre was visiting. They had gone away somewhere, but I did not know where as she had not told me. She didn't even tell me when she would return. I feared for our friendship and wished she was here and it was as it had been for those first few weeks after we met.

I continued as normal, my daily routine rarely varying. Another girl, Petra, who normally worked part-time, was brought in to cover Rebecca's shifts. Petra was Polish. She was polite, spoke very little English, and was eager to work. But she seemed to have no interest in forming friendships with anyone in the hotel. She had a boyfriend and, on more than one occasion, I saw him outside the hotel, smoking and constantly checking his watch as he waited for her to finish work.

How I longed to talk to someone. My heart ached to unload my troubles into a friendly ear. But there was no one, only Rebecca, and she was not there for me. I spent my lunch hours wandering the city streets like a lost soul. I pushed my way through masses of people. Hundreds, maybe thousands passed me, but their glares were distant, and despite the crowds, I was lonely—I was, in effect, a ghost that strayed unseen and unheard amid the multitude.

I sat on the cool grass that blanketed the hill overlooking the pond in Stephen's Green. My thoughts wandered from one thing to another, but kept coming back to the name that was niggling away in the back of my mind—Robert Cleary. I was curious about him. Why wouldn't I be? Despite Grandma's disclosures, I could not think of him in terms of being my *real* father. My real father was a black-and-white photograph on the mantelpiece in our old house back in Sligo. The picture had a gold-coloured frame around it and the glass was stained a light shade of yellow from sitting close to the fire. I grew up looking at his face that would remain forever young and I grew to love the man that I was too young to retain memories of. While I may have been too young to remember him, he was nevertheless my father. There were occasions when I entered the sitting room unexpectedly and found Mother sitting in the armchair, the framed photo grasped between her folded arms. Her eyes would be red and her cheeks damp and glistening in the orange glow from the fire. She would wave me closer and hug me with all her might, but without ever speaking a word. He was the only father I had, even if he was not there when I was a child. I had often cried alone in my room, wishing for his presence.

But the name Robert Cleary would not go away. No matter how hard I tried, I could not dispel the seed of curiosity that was growing within me. I wondered if seeing him would satisfy that curiosity. Would that be enough to make me forget his name and move on? Would I feel a need to talk to him? I didn't think I would. What would I say? *Hello, Mr Cleary, I'm Anna, your daughter.* Or maybe more fitting, *Hello, you bastard, do you have any idea of what my mother went through because of your lustful desires?* No, I decided, I did not want to, and would probably be unable to confront him. But would I like to see him, just to see what he looked like? Maybe I looked like him.

Grandma said he was transferred to another school, but where? And that was eighteen years ago. He could be anywhere in the country now, and maybe even abroad. Having no idea how I would go about finding him, I decided to leave it for the moment, and maybe even forever.

"Are you all right, my dear?" Grandma asked.

I looked up as she placed a bowl of coddle in front of me. "Yes, Gran, I'm fine."

"I've been so worried," she said, her face etched with concern. "I hope I did the right thing in telling you."

"I'm fine, Gran, honestly. You don't have to worry about me."

"Good." She nodded, a degree of relief easing her worried expression.

The kitchen door swung open and Peter came in. His appearance startled me. He had just crawled out of bed, even though it was seven in the evening. His eyes were bloodshot and his face was dotted with blotchy red patches. The stale stench of beer entered the room with him. His clothes were rumpled, giving him a dishevelled appearance, like a hobo that had been sleeping out in the fields.

"Hello, Peter," I said.

"Hi ya," he replied in a hoarse voice, his facial lines crunching up as if speaking seemed to cause pain.

"Sit here, Peter," Grandma said, indicating his place by setting out a knife and fork.

He sat down and rubbed the back of his head in an apparent attempt to ease his hangover.

Grandma took a plate that had been sitting on top of a pot of boiling water. She removed the lid that was covering the plate and placed his dinner in front of him. It was a sorry-looking meal and looked as if it had been made yesterday and only now reheated. On the plate were a pork chop, mashed potatoes, and mushy peas. The meat was shrivelled to half its original size. I watched as he struggled to cut into it. It was tough, like a strip of old leather. The peas looked likewise, dry and devoid of moisture. The potatoes no longer had a look of whiteness about them. Their edges were tainted in a greenish colour as they hardened. He seemed unfazed by the quality of the meal and gorged down the food like a half-starved man. Grandma fussed about him as if he was a helpless child, filling his cup, buttering his bread, and generally seeing he wanted for nothing.

Peter never thanked her or even acknowledged the fact

that she was there, waiting on him hand and foot. She didn't seem bothered by his display of ungratefulness, and was simply content to know his needs were tended to.

The noise of the front door opening and then being pulled shut told me Grandpa was home. Neither Peter nor Grandma showed any reaction, but my stomach churned with dread of seeing him. He walked into the kitchen, and his first act was to give Peter a look of disapproval. He muttered something under his breath, but Peter ignored him.

"Do you want a cup of tea?" Grandma asked him.

"Yes," he said, and just like Peter, did not bother to thank her. He glanced at me for a moment, but said nothing.

I looked down, unable to hold his glare even for those few seconds. Grandma placed a mug of tea in front of him and he muttered something in the way of thanks, but I did not catch his words.

Peter, having finished his dinner, showed a sudden look of realisation as something came to mind. "Did you get the message?" he asked me.

"What message?"

"A girl called for you a short while ago. I heard a knock on the door. Someone answered and I heard her asking for you. I looked out the window and saw her walking away. Nice-looking girl...at least from behind," he said, smiling.

I looked at my grandparents, wondering which one of them had answered the door.

"Nice girls don't wear skirts that display more than they cover," Grandpa said with venom, almost spitting in disgust as he spoke.

"Was it my friend, Rebecca?" I asked, excited at the thought of seeing her again.

"I don't think she's a fitting friend for you," Grandpa said.

I looked at him, confused, not sure how to reply to such a silly statement.

"She works with Anna. Doesn't she, Anna?" Grandma said.

I was both surprised and impressed in a grateful sort of way that she had spoken. It had been her normal practice to remain silent when Grandpa was being boorish.

"Yes," I said. "She is my friend and she has been good to me."

"What's wrong with her?" Grandma asked him.

"She's common, that's what's wrong with her."

"Common?" I said, in such a way that made clear I wanted him to explain. I believe I was gaining courage from Grandma.

"Yes, common. You listen to me, young woman." His voice raised and he pointed his finger at me. Small veins on his forehead bulged. "You know nothing of city life. You're a young, foolish girl that would be easily led in the wrong company."

I remained silent, intimidated by his manner, but Grandma tried to calm his rant. "She's not—"

"You keep quiet, woman, this is not your business." He snapped at her without taking his intense glare from me. "Listen to me, Anna," he said, or rather demanded, and it was the first time he'd used my name. "I know what I'm talking about. If you associate with the wrong sort, you'll end up in trouble just like your mother."

I wanted to stand up and run, but my legs felt as if they had turned into dead weights made of lead. So I sat quietly, listening to his vile outpouring of vicious hatred. At that moment, I hated myself. I hated myself for not having the courage to stand up and denounce him for the pig he was. How dare he speak in derogatory terms about my mother? His outpouring of contemptible words continued to flow, but I did not hear them anymore. Nobody was listening to him as he ranted and raved.

There were people I'd disliked in my life. It was only natural to meet people I was unable to bond with. But Grandpa was the first person I hated, truly hated.

Thirteen

I pressed the bell that was labelled number eight. Within seconds, Rebecca's cheery face appeared out the top window. She disappeared for a brief moment before reappearing and dangling the door keys in an outstretched arm. She dropped the small bunch of keys and I caught them before they hit the pavement, which surprised me as my eye and hand coordination was usually clumsy.

I let myself in and made my way up the four flights of stairs. Different noises met me on each landing. On the first, a baby cried while other children talked loudly as if engaging in an animated game. Mingled with the young voices was the sound of the baby's mother trying to soothe the crying infant with a lullaby. On the second landing there was the clanging of pots and cutlery bashing against each other and the sound of two men in a heated but controlled debate. A woman's voice sounded as if she was trying to engage in the lively discussion, but her words were drowned out by the louder male voices. On the second to last landing, a young couple talked in low voices, almost whispering to each another. They had just come out of one of the flats and he was pulling the door closed behind them. They glanced around nervously when they heard my footsteps on the stairs. I stood to one side to let them pass and they neither thanked me nor turned sideways to make passing on the stairs easier. They were no older than I was and both had a similar look of gauntness in their faces. Their eyes were dark, as if the eyeballs were sinking back into their skulls. Although they had not said or done anything, I was glad to get past them and find myself on the top landing.

I entered Rebecca's flat a little breathless and was greeted with the warmest of hugs. Her strong embrace dispelled any worries I had about our friendship. We sat on the side of the bed with mugs of coffee and began to catch up on everything that had happened since we last saw each another. I held back the news about my real father while she excitedly told me about her relationship with Pierre.

"He adores me, Anna, he absolutely adores me. Have you ever had a man that adored you?"

"No," I said, thinking back to past boyfriends. They were boys and not men, and like all teenage boys, would not know what true love was.

"I think he's going to ask me to go to France with him," she said, struggling to hold in the excitement of the thought.

"France?" I said, or rather blurted out in disbelief.

She nodded, unable to contain her smile.

"You mean...forever?" I asked.

She nodded again, the smile having not left her face.

"What makes you think he'll ask?"

"What else can he do?" She held out her arms as if it was obvious. "In a month or two, his work in Ireland will be finished. He'll still have to visit occasionally, but not as often, maybe just once or twice a year."

"And you think in a couple of months, he won't be able to leave you behind?"

"How can he? He loves me and said he can't live without me. So I don't see any other option for him, do you?"

I thought for a moment before answering. "No, not if he truly loves you."

"And he does," she said instantly.

"But do you love him?"

"Hmm..." She pondered on my question for a while. There was no look of embarrassment at not being able to answer without thought. "I do like him, like him a lot, but love? That might be too strong a word to describe my feelings for him."

"But how can you marry a man you don't love?" I asked.

"Oh, Anna, my friend, you really can be naive sometimes." She looked at me as if I was a silly child. "People get married for all sorts of reasons and love is just one of them."

"But to commit yourself to someone for the rest of your

life when you don't love them? I mean, is *liking* someone enough?" I think I was asking myself the question as much as I was asking her.

"The rest of my life seems like a long time. I don't want to think that far ahead. All I know is I'm happy when I'm with him and he *does* love me."

We made more coffee and continued to talk about Pierre, France, and the wonderful life that lay ahead for her. There was a niggling suspicion in the back of my mind that regardless of what Pierre may have told her, he was intending to return home alone and had no intentions of including Rebecca in his future. But suspicions were all they were, so I kept them to myself. I knew mentioning them would serve no other purpose than to drive a wedge between the two of us.

After a while, Rebecca changed the subject. "So, what's been happening with you these past few weeks?"

My normal reply to such a question would be, *Oh, not much*, but for once, I hardly knew where to begin. *My Uncle Peter is drinking himself to death. My Gran has confirmed my suspicions about Grandfather being a tyrant. Oh, and I've discovered that my father was not my father after all.*

I decided to tell her about my day out with Grandma, and relayed the whole conversation we had when she revealed the truth about my fathers. Yes, I used the word fathers, because that was how my confused mind felt, that I had two.

Rebecca was astounded and left speechless for a few seconds, but it was long enough for her jaw to drop as an indication of her amazement about my news. I think it was my casual manner in explaining the story as much as the story itself that stunned her.

"You've got to find him," she finally said.

"Why?" It was a stupid reply. Deep down I knew I wanted to see this faceless man, but for some reason, I felt a need to be talked into it.

"Why! Are you kidding me? This guy is your real father. You have to track him down. Otherwise you'll go through life wondering what he is like."

"I don't know," I said, shrugging. Naturally, I knew she was right and had no idea why I pretended to be indifferent about it.

"Anna, if I knew where to find my parents, do you think I'd be sitting here now?"

"Your parents are still alive?" I had assumed she was an orphan.

"I don't know...not for sure anyway. To be honest, I don't really know anything. Before the nuns shoved me out the door, I did ask about them."

"And what did they tell you?"

"They told me nothing, just spurted out words such as confidentiality and privacy."

"I'm sorry, Rebecca. I feel guilty now."

"About what?"

"Here am I going on about having two fathers and not even being bothered to look up my real one. And here you are, not knowing if yours are alive or dead."

"Don't be silly," she said, reaching out to rub my arm. "If I was to begrudge every person that had a parent, I'd be a pretty miserable person by now, don't you think?" She laughed, and I laughed with her, happy that we were so close we could share anything.

"So, what are you going to do?" she asked.

"I don't know. I wouldn't have the first idea how to go about tracking him down."

"Eh..." She looked at me as if I was stupid. "What about the phone directory?"

It was such an obvious idea that I silently berated myself for not thinking of it. *Surely it can't be that simple,* I thought. "But maybe he's not listed? Maybe he's not even living in Dublin anymore?"

"You won't know unless you try. Hold on, I'll be back in a minute." She stood and left the room.

I listened to her feet thumping down the stairs at high speed. It sounded like she was skipping three steps at a time. I knew where she was going. There was a pay phone down in the hall and I had seen several phone books stacked on a wooden shelf below it. She arrived back, red-faced and breathing heavily. Under her arm was the directory for Dublin City.

We sat cross-legged on the floor and thumbed through the pages. Rebecca slowed and then stopped at the surname Cleary. Her finger traced a path down the page, following the Christian names until she came to Robert Cleary. There were five entries under that name and two more listed as R. Cleary. I looked at the addresses. They were scattered roughly equal across the city. Three were southside, two northside, and two in the city centre.

"What now?" I asked.

"We phone them, I suppose," she said, looking up at me. "Let's see if one of them is the guy you want, and then...well, that's up to you."

"Phone them? What would I say? Hello, I might be your daughter. Did you seduce my mother eighteen years ago?"

Rebecca laughed at the thought of such a conversation. Then she composed herself and surprised me with her cunning.

"We'll phone them one at a time and say we are from the Teachers' Union of Ireland and are updating our records. We just want to confirm their name and address, which we will already know from the book. We'll know from their reaction if they are a teacher, what do you think?"

"Okay," I said reluctantly. I could feel a nervousness spreading through my body at the thought of actually making contact. "Will you make the calls? I don't think I'll have the nerve to do it."

"Yes, I can do that," she said with a smile and an air of confidence that made me envious. "But not now, it's far too late to be phoning people."

I looked at my watch. It was gone midnight. I had not noticed the hours slipping by.

"We'll make the calls tomorrow, as soon as we finish work," she said.

I nodded, unable to shake the sick feeling in my stomach. "I better go." It was late and if I didn't go to bed soon, I would struggle to get up for work in the morning.

"Why don't you stay? I can make up a bed on the floor for you."

I thought about it, and it was tempting. The room was warm and cosy, heated by the turf fire that was still blazing. "I better not. Grandma will be worried if I don't come home."

I left, and shivered as the cold of the night wrapped itself around me like a blanket of ice. The roads were desolate and for the first time in Dublin, I felt scared and vulnerable. I walked quickly, keeping to the main road where the glare of street lamps gave some solace to my feeling of solitude.

When I got home, the house was quiet and I climbed into my bed where the cold sheets gave me little comfort. I was tired, but a mixture of fear and excitement prevented me from sleeping for quite a while. I dreamed as I often did. Crazy dreams that made no sense seemed to occupy my thoughts. I woke when I heard the clanging of milk bottles being placed on the doorstep. I lay motionless and listened to the hum of the milkman's cart stopping and starting as he worked his way along the street. I looked at the clock and closed my eyes, hoping to make the most of the forty-five minutes left before my day would begin.

Fourteen

I never knew a work day to pass so slowly. Whenever I looked at my watch, only minutes had passed since my last glance. We finished early, but still had to wait until six o'clock before we could leave. We spent the final hour sitting in the staff restroom waiting for our shift to end. It was a basic room with an old sofa and a few plastic chairs. There was a small wobbly table with a kettle and a bottle of milk to make tea if we wanted. There was no fridge and the milk was always warm and always seemed to be on the verge of turning sour.

Rebecca lay dozing on the sofa while I sat in boredom on one of the chairs. There was little to do other than look at the wall clock or the tourism calendar that hung crookedly next to it. I hated that calendar, for what reason I cannot explain. Maybe it was the annoying cheery faces of hotel staff smiling down at me. Or possibly it was the fact it always displayed the previous month. Nobody seemed bothered, including me, to turn the page at the beginning of each new month. Although, someone would give in at some point, albeit a couple of weeks late.

So I watched the clock. It was one of those cheap ones that could be bought in any knickknack shop. It had a drab, cream-coloured face surrounded by a white plastic frame. My attention was on the second hand. It seemed to drag itself around with deliberate sluggishness. I knew it was my imagination, but the thin black pointer appeared to slow down as it made the uphill journey toward twelve. I stared with despair at its slow progress. My pointless attempts of using willpower to speed it up only seemed to have the opposite effect.

Armed with a pocketful of change, I dialled the first number in the book. The moment I heard the ringing tone, I passed the handset to Rebecca. I knew I would freeze when it came time to speak. What did surprise me was the ease in which her voice and complete manner changed when the phone was answered. I listened as she transformed into a slightly snooty and efficient secretary.

"Hello, am I speaking to Mr Cleary? Good evening, Mr Cleary, this is Miss Jacobs from the Teachers' Union of Ireland. I wonder if I could have a moment of your time to confirm some of your details as listed on the Register of Teachers?"

Her change of expression made it plain to me the man on the other end of the line was voicing his confusion.

"Oh, I'm terribly sorry, I seem to have dialled the wrong number," she said quite rapidly, and hung up without giving the bewildered man a chance to say anything else.

"You can cross him off," she said to me.

I read out the second number and she dialled each digit as I called it out. The conversation followed much the same lines as the first call and accordingly, I crossed out the second name on the page.

There was no reply from the next two entries, which left three to go. I rang a Mr R Cleary that lived on the north side of the city. I didn't hold out much hope of it being the man we were seeking. To be honest, I did not know if I was relieved or disappointed at our lack of success. I was in the process of trying to decide which way I felt when Rebecca's words to the fifth person on the list caused me to freeze.

"Thank you, Mr Cleary. We just need to check a few details as we are trying to update our register."

She grabbed my arm for a moment and then withdrew her hand to give one of those maybe, maybe not, waving movements.

"We have your address down as number one, Hollybank Road, is that correct? Okay, great," she said after he obviously confirmed the address. Of course, she was reading it from the phone book, but her knowledge of his details was putting credence to her assumed identity. "And our records show you are teaching at Our Lady of Charity in Stanhope Street?"

There were a few seconds of silence and then Rebecca's expression changed to one of great concentration as she listened to what he was saying. I could not hear his words, only a muffled voice coming from the speaker, so I was only getting her side of the conversation.

"Seventeen years ago?" she said, repeating snippets of his speech. "Oh my, some of our records are badly out of date." She let him say something and then asked, "So, where are you teaching now, Mr Cleary?" She grabbed the pencil and scribbled a school's name on the corner of the page. As she thanked him and said goodbye, I turned the book around to read what she had written. It read, Our lady of Victories, Beaumont Road.

We made our way back up to Rebecca's flat. I don't remember the steps or lifting my feet to take each one in turn as I seemed to be functioning on some sort of autopilot. To say I felt sick with fear would go nowhere near describing my emotions. My head was swimming with confusion. Suddenly, this faceless man had become real. He had been there only seconds ago at the other end of the phone. I knew his address. It was little more than a twenty minute walk from Ignatius Road. I could jump on a bus and travel to his house in five. I could knock on his door and, when he answered, there he would be, not two feet away standing in the doorway and looking at me—my biological father. But what if he did not open the door? What if his wife did? Did he have a wife? What if a boy or girl opened the door? Surely he had children over the years.

Then it dawned on me—maybe I had a brother or sister I never knew existed. I thought about that for a while, and the thought they might exist sent a strange wave of muddled thoughts spinning around my head. I grew up as an only child, but I was never particularly lonely. All right, that's not strictly true. As a young child, I did yearn for a sister to play with, but as I got older, I developed an acceptance of my situation and became quite content with my own company. But now I was older. Did I really want a sister? My mind reeled with the conflict between the possibility of not being alone and the reason for what should be a happy thought— that the man responsible was probably the person I should hate more than anyone else in this world.

I sat thinking while Rebecca made us something to eat.

My head ached and I wished the whole sorry mess would just go away as if it never happened. At my request, Rebecca stopped talking about my father. I needed time to come to terms with what we discovered. I was unsure about what to do and decided to wait in the belief that in a few days, I might think more clearly about the whole thing. At least, that was my hope.

I arrived home to find Grandma alone and in tears. She was sitting at the kitchen table wiping her eyes dry. She looked up at me with a pitiful expression.

"Grandma, what's wrong?" I sat down and put my arm around her shoulder.

"Oh, Anna, my sweet grandchild, I thought you would be home hours ago."

"I went to Rebecca's after work. I told you yesterday I would not be home until late. Don't you remember, Grandma?"

"Did you? I'm sorry, my child, my memory is not so good these days."

"Is that why you are upset, because I did not come home?"

"No, that's not why I was crying." She gave her eyes another wipe, this time exaggerating the movement in the belief it would help prevent further tears.

"What's happened, Grandma? Tell me."

"It's Peter and your grandfather."

"What about them? What happened?"

"They had a terrible argument this morning. They were shouting and I thought it might have turned to fisticuffs. I've never seen Peter so angry."

"What were they arguing about?"

"Grandpa told Peter if he did not get a job, he was to get out. But it was more than that, it was the language he used. He called Peter some terrible things."

She reached out for the tissues again and I pushed the box closer to her. I watched her hand tremble as she lifted the hanky to her eyes. Her gaunt face was white, as if she were a ghost of some kind.

"Where are they now?" I asked.

"Patrick went to his club a while ago."

"And Peter?"

"I don't know. He left after the argument and I haven't seen him since this morning." She looked at me, her eyes red and swollen. "I'm worried about him, Anna. I'm so worried."

I squeezed her hand and tried to console her. "Don't upset yourself, Grandma. He'll come home when he's ready, and I'm sure he will have calmed down."

"You don't understand, my child, you don't know what kind of man your uncle Peter is."

"Tell me, Grandma. Tell me so I can understand."

"Peter is harmless, but when he drinks, he changes. He'll get himself into trouble. I just know he will."

"Did he have money for drink when he left?"

"Yes, he had a lot of money. That's why I'm worried."

"Where did he get the money?"

"He had a big win on the horses yesterday. You did not know he betted on the horses, did you, Anna?"

I shook my head.

"Oh yes, mostly he loses, but sometimes he wins, and sometimes he wins a lot of money."

"Do you want me to look for him, Grandma?"

Her face softened; a small glimmer of hope sparkled in her eyes. I no more wanted to leave the house searching for my drunken uncle, but her pitiful look made it impossible for me not to offer.

"Will you, Anna? Will you do that for me?"

"Of course I will, Grandma." I squeezed her hand a little tighter. It was her I would do it for, not for Peter, but for her. "Do you have any idea where he might be?"

"When Peter has money, he usually goes to the bars near the fruit and vegetable markets. They stay open very late, sometimes all night."

"I will find him, Grandma, don't you worry."

I closed up my coat and she shoved money into my pocket as I walked toward the front door.

"Get a taxi, Anna. It's too late for a girl to walk the streets, and the buses will not be running at this hour."

I kissed her on the cheek and went back out into the cold night air.

Fifteen

Dorset Street acquired a different atmosphere after dark. The small shops dotting the road all the way into town were closed. Their windows, each with its own character, were hidden behind graffiti-covered shutters and grills. The cheerful faces of storekeepers and customers alike were swapped for grotesque attempts of art hastily sprayed onto the grey metal shutters with aerosol cans. The hubbub of business along with the laughter and chatter of people was gone. In its place, the lonely rattle of metal shutters flexed in the wind. The odd car passed and went all the faster now that the road was quiet. The rumble of their engines pierced the night air and the drone of noisy exhausts could be heard long after the cars disappeared from sight.

I stood close to the curb and looked up and down the road, but there were no signs of any taxis. The city was always quiet on midweek nights, as many were waiting for payday at the weekend before they could afford to go out. The lack of taxis reflected this, with most drivers preferring to save their petrol for Friday and Saturday when they knew they would be busy.

I began to walk. I knew the markets and it would only take about twenty minutes on foot. The wind had turned chilly and I kept my fingers warm by pushing my hands deep into my coat pockets. I walked at a brisk pace, anxious to find less lonely streets where the feeling of isolation would not be so intense. I was not particularly worried, but there was something unsettling about walking along deserted streets. The noise of one's footsteps seemed almost deafening and should a person stop for a moment, the echo of pounding feet would last for a few seconds. It was an unnerving sound that made a person believe they were being followed, even though they knew they were the source of the eerie footsteps lingering in the shadows of the night. The wind did not help, even if it was just a light breeze. In fact, the lighter the wind, the worse it seemed. A strong breeze occupied one's mind as they battled to walk into it, and the rush of gusting air blanketed all those intimidating sounds of the night.

I continued on, through the glow of street lamps that seemed stuck somewhere between steady and flickering as the poles swayed ever so slightly.

It was with some relief when I left the loneliness of Dorset Street and found myself walking along Capel Street toward the river. The street had many pubs and a few late night clubs, and despite being midweek, there were people scattered about here and there. I passed one public house after another. As I walked by each door, voices, laughter, and folk music resounded from within. I got a blast of cigarette smoke if a door happened to open at the moment I passed. Several times I stepped aside as drunken revellers stumbled from doorways. After regaining their balance, they stood motionless and stared blankly up and down the road, trying to get their bearings. Having determined the way to go, they adopted the most ridiculous postures as they staggered along the footpath.

I left Capel Street for the narrow cobblestoned roads of Smithfield. I instantly became sorry I had not found a taxi to take me to the markets. Without any lighting, the roads were pitch black. I quickened my step, while at the same time began to get the smell of rotting vegetables in the air.

I wandered the old lanes of Dublin. The area was packed with small depots and warehouses that would burst into chaotic life before dawn when trucks arrived from the port, their containers crammed with fresh vegetables and fruit of every sort from Europe. The area would then become bedlam as fresh food was sold and distributed to waiting vans that would disperse them around the city. Street traders would also converge on the area, pushing carts and old prams, looking for bargains they could sell on street corners. I continued to walk as I looked for pubs. I began to regret my offer to look for Peter. I had no idea where he might be, if indeed he was here at all.

The first pub I came across was nestled between two boarded up buildings. The two floors above it had a vacant and derelict appearance. The windows were broken and shards of glass were sticking out of the frames, looking menacingly dangerous. Torn curtains waved out the gaps in a ghostly manner. There was no noise as I approached the doorway and I got the feeling there would be no one inside. Perhaps, despite the dull light shining from within, the premises would be as desolate as the buildings that surrounded it.

I smelt the strong, pungent odour of stout as I approached the door. The sweet, sharp tang of oats and barley filled my nostrils when I stepped into the entrance lobby. When I pushed open the inner door, I was met with a sombre scene.

Besides the man behind the bar, there were about ten customers, all old men and all with dark pints of Guinness before them. There was no conversation. The only noise was from a small portable television sitting precariously on a shelf behind the counter. The crackle of static from it ensured the voices from the set were inaudible. None of the customers seemed bothered by the dreadful noise, and the bartender was preoccupied by a stubborn spot of dirt that had fixed itself to the bottom of a glass.

It was as if every glass of stout held its owner in some sort of trance. Each man appeared to be mimicking one another in their devotion to the drink before them. There they sat, each and every one of them, in silence, in reverence, captivated by the majestic crown of white foam sitting proudly upon the black liquid. After a moment, a hand would reach out, its fingers wrapping themselves firmly around the glass. The glass would then rise to the lips of the man holding it. An indescribable look of inner pleasure would spread across his face, and his Adam's apple would twitch as he gulped down a mouthful. The glass would return to its exact spot and the man would resume his lonely trance-like posture.

The bartender was the only one to look in my direction, and it was only for the briefest of moments. His attention soon went back to the bar towel he was turning around the inside of the stained glass. Satisfying myself Peter was not there, I left, slipping out the door as unnoticed as I had entered.

There was another pub around the corner and it was not much different from the previous one. I began to lose hope of finding him and wondered if at that moment he was already home. I could picture the scene—the fire blazing and Peter warming his hands while Grandma fussed about him with mugs of tea and warm toast.

I continued along the old tramlines, unsure which way to go. I found myself entering the seedier side of Dublin. As I neared the tall, grey walls of the army barracks, I saw women flaunting themselves to passing cars that slowed as drivers visually inspected the goods on sale. There was nothing glamorous in what I saw. The crudely painted faces of the women were sad and wreaked of desperation. I turned to walk back in the direction I came from, feeling intimidated by various men that lurked in the shadows, their presence all the more obvious by their vain attempts to look natural in the most sleaziest of locations.

The night was only getting later and I was accomplishing nothing other than wasting my time. I turned for home, but shouting in the distance grabbed my attention.

I turned to see a man standing in the street. He was facing a doorway and was engaged in a shouting match with someone inside, although from my angle, I could not see the door. I knew the voice and squinted as I tried to penetrate the darkness. He continued to shout, his hoarse bellows sounding amplified in the quiet night air. His arms waved above his head, adding animation to his anger. It was Peter. If I had not recognised the familiar voice, I would surely have known his distinctive stocky build, even in the half-light.

I walked toward him, and as I did, there was a loud bang as the door slammed shut. This enraged Peter even more and he threw himself at the door, pounding his great big fists against it. He did not see me approach. I stood well back and called out his name. The racket of his fists hammering the wooden door drowned out my voice. I called out again and then a third time, my voice raised to an uncharacteristic scream that was powered from my timid lungs. He turned to face me. His eyes were wild with a madness I had never seen in anyone before, and it frightened me.

"The cheating bastards took my money!" he roared at me. His expression showed no surprise I was even there, as unexpected as it was.

"Who did?"

"Those bastards in there!" he yelled, and turned to place his foot squarely in the centre of the door. The noise of his heavy boot slamming into the wood panelling was like a shotgun blast and the clatter echoed as it rebounded against the buildings lining the narrow road. The door shook violently and the hinges strained in the frame, but they stood fast and the door held.

He took a couple steps backwards as he prepared to launch another assault with his boot. I stepped forward and grabbed his arm.

"Peter, please come home. Grandma is worried about you."

My words fell on deaf ears. In his enraged state of mind, he could hear nothing but the demons in his head. He lurched forward again, my grip on his coat breaking with the force of his body surging forward. The clatter of the door shaking in its frame was immense, and I was amazed that despite its obvious sturdiness, it did not cave in. Peter staggered backwards, unsteady on his feet. His look of disappointment and the fact he was limping gave me hope that he would give up.

"Peter, let's go. I'm sure someone will have called the Gardaí by now."

He nodded as he turned. I don't think my mentioning the Gardaí worried him at all. No, it was a case that his strength was exhausted and he hurt his leg, although he tried hard not to show it. We walked toward the quays to find a taxi, and Peter's anger slowly ebbed away like a receding tide. By the time we found ourselves sitting in the back of a taxi, he had gone quiet, so quiet that for a moment I thought he had dozed off with the dry heat blowing from the dashboard's air vents.

As always, Grandma stayed up to wait for him to come home. He sat like an ungrateful lord at the fire while she tended his every need. I stayed in the kitchen and made my own tea. The heat of the mug stung my hands, but it was a pleasurable pain. I gathered from Grandma that the house where I found him was a gambling house. And so it was that all the money he won on a horse, he lost on the turn of a card. Grandma seemed confident he'd learnt his lesson and would not be so foolish with his money again. I did not have the heart to tell her that she was deluding herself.

$\mathcal{S}$ixteen

I felt like a thief in the night, lurking in the shadows trying to steal a glimpse of someone I did not know and had never met but, nevertheless, was responsible for my very existence. I might have fooled Rebecca into thinking I was not interested in my biological father, but I did not fool myself. A deep-rooted longing to know where I came from had gotten the better of me. It woke me from my sleep. It tormented my thoughts until I could resist no longer. It dragged me from the house as the clock in the hall struck midnight, and after a twenty minute walk, it brought me to Hollybank Road, where the man I believed might be my real father lived. I stood against the thick trunk of a large willow tree, its branches drooping down, almost to head height. The swaying foliage surrounded me like an umbrella provided by Mother Nature, and along with the cold, damp air, the smell of wet leaves and soggy wood filled my nostrils. The house opposite me was in darkness and I wondered if I was truly sane or perhaps warped like a crazed stalker. For that was how I felt, hiding in the dark, watching and waiting.

After thirty minutes of nothing happening, the realisation of my stupidity got the better of me and I walked away. No sooner had I reached the corner of the street when a car door slamming shattered the silence of night. I turned to see a taxi outside the house. A man and a woman had gotten out. She was already standing at the front door of number one and was waiting for the man. He was handing money to the driver through the open passenger window.

I hurried back, walking as fast as I could without running, which might draw attention to me. But I was too late to get a good look. After paying the fare, the man reached the door in just a few steps and they disappeared into the house. I cursed myself for having walked away, but then thought maybe it was for the best. Perhaps it was fate telling me I was better off forgetting the man that lived on Hollybank Road. Nobody knew, including myself, what sort of trouble I would be both inviting and inflicting by making my presence known. I walked home, steeped in despondency, despite knowing it was probably for the best.

The following day, I shared the exploits of my midnight excursion with Rebecca. She was the only one I could tell, the only one I dared tell. In her, I could confide my feelings, my confusion, and the mental turmoil that would not go away. But as I talked, I sensed some indifference in her re-action and her replies. Gone was the overflowing enthusiasm she normally bristled with. She did try to show interest, but her bubbly nature was dampened. By what, I did not know. I could see it in her eyes. They were heavy with thought and, when she looked at me, her glare was somewhere else.

"What's wrong, Rebecca?"

"Nothing, why do you ask?"

"You seem preoccupied."

"Oh for heaven's sake, Anna. Maybe I have problems of my own. Maybe the world does not revolve around you. Did you ever consider that?"

I did not answer. I was taken aback by her abruptness and did not know what to say.

"Oh I'm sorry, Anna." She reached out to grab my hand. "That was a terrible thing for me to say. I don't know why I said it."

"It's all right," I said. "I do tend to go on sometimes about my own problems."

"No, it's not all right. You are my friend, my best friend. It's just that..." Her words trailed off. It was obvious she wanted to tell me something, but for some reason, was una-ble to.

"How are things going with Pierre?"

She did not speak, instead choosing to shrug and exhale in an exaggerated manner.

"Has he said anything about leaving Ireland?"

Again, I got a similar reply, consisting of various body movements that displayed apathy.

Well, I didn't need her to explain it to me. She did not want to talk about it, which meant the relationship was not progressing as planned— planned by Rebecca, that is.

The next few weeks held little in the way of change as far as Rebecca's enthusiasm for Pierre. If anything, she seemed to display more and more indifference toward the relationship. Her attitude confused me because she still spent most of her spare time in his company. It was only when he was away that I would see her outside of work. During those times together, she rarely mentioned his name, only doing so if he happened to be connected to whatever she was talking about in the first place. She would never bring him up as the main topic of conversation as she had constantly done in the beginning.

I think one of the reasons my mind kept returning to the teacher, Robert Cleary, was because I was lonely. I felt unable to share my feelings with anyone other than Rebecca, but she was preoccupied with her own thoughts of late, thoughts she was not sharing with me.

With time on my hands, I continually found myself in Drumcondra, wandering around Tolka Park, or buying something trivial in one of the shops opposite St Patrick's Teaching College. I told myself I was simply walking for something to do and it was either Drumcondra or the other direction, which led into the city centre, and that was a direction I walked every day to and from work. But despite refusing to admit it, I knew why I was there. Perhaps I would get a look at him as he came or went from the house. Maybe if he walked to the shop, I could follow him, stand behind him in the queue. Perhaps I could even say something as we waited to be served, the type of comment strangers make for no particular reason other than to pass the time of day.

I knew there was an unhealthy preoccupation growing inside of me over Robert Cleary, but I could not shake the urge to see him, even if only from a distance. Although I would not admit it to myself, I knew that would not be enough. If I saw him, the next step would be to say something to him. I cursed my own curiosity and wished I could leave well enough alone. But I knew I wouldn't.

Seventeen

Rebecca never suspected and I felt bad lying to her. I consoled my conscience with the thought that it was for her own good. *The lie?* I had to take a half day from work as I had arranged a dentist appointment. *The truth?* I knew Pierre left the hotel most days at midday to wander around the city. He was usually gone for about an hour, sometimes two. It was my plan to talk to him, to try and find out what was happening between him and Rebecca. It was not nosiness, for I was never preoccupied with the affairs of others. I was worried about my friend and felt justified in doing something that might help.

Pierre Beaufort was a creature of habit and, true to form, at twelve o'clock, he walked out of the hotel. I was across the road intermingling with people studying the colourful movie posters adorning the walls of the Savoy Cinema. The throngs of people, some walking and some hurrying along O'Connell Street, ensured I was invisible in the crowd.

For the next half hour, I remained hidden while he walked, pausing only to glance in shop windows. I followed from a safe distance, knowing the chance of him seeing me was remote. Never before had I felt so devious, but my actions were for the greater good.

I continued to trail Pierre as he strolled like a man without a care in the world. All I could do was watch and wait; wait for the right opportunity to present itself.

I became aware of how much one can learn about another's character by simply observing. A beggar sat cross-legged in the doorway of a vacant shop. Pierre saw him and stopped to rummage for change, which he tossed into the paper cup that was being held out by the tramp. He slowed whenever passing an off-licence, staring intently at the stacked bottles of wine as if trying to focus on the small print of the labels.

We crossed the Liffey and wound our way through the narrow and atmospheric lanes of Temple Bar. Pierre seemed mesmerized any time he passed an art shop. He'd stand looking in the window as if held in awe at the paintings on display. Twice he walked into such stores with such a look of determination I was convinced he would be coming out with neatly wrapped canvases under both arms.

After half an hour, my legs were tired and I considered turning around, thinking a suitable moment to approach him would never present itself. But as the thought was floating around my mind, he sat down at an outside table of an Italian bistro. I ducked into a newsagent and hovered around the newspapers as I watched through the front window. A waitress appeared, but he waved away the menu, seemingly already knowing what he wanted.

"It's now or never," I said under my breath and decided to act quickly before the knot in my stomach grew tighter and dissuaded me from my mission. I bought a paper before leaving the shop, thinking by carrying it I would look even more inconspicuous.

I crossed the road and walked toward the cafe. I hoped he'd believe he saw me first. And he did. I was thirty feet away when he peered out over the rim of his sunglasses. His hand rose into the air and a smile spread across his face. I waited a few seconds before displaying the realisation of recognizing the stranger, which I deemed appropriative if I wanted him to believe the meeting was pure chance.

"Hello, Anna, are you not working today?" He continued to smile as he spoke and then stood to pull out a chair for me. To an observer's eyes, it must have looked like a prearranged meeting.

"No," I said. "I had to go to the dentist today, so I took the afternoon off." I was never good at lying, but my lack of embarrassment and the realisation that my face had not blown up in a bright red colour surprised me. Perhaps I was developing the art of deception through practice.

The waitress appeared with a cappuccino and Pierre said

something to her in Italian. The words flowed from his lips with effortless fluency and I could not help but be impressed, although I tried not to show it. They both looked at me, and he asked what I would like to drink.

"Just tea," I said, feeling terribly uncosmopolitan.

"Un tè, per piacere," he said to the girl.

The waitress turned and left us.

"I hope your visit to the dentist did not hurt?"

"Oh no, it was just a filling." I reached up to tip my left cheek and made a mental note to remember which side I was touching.

I almost froze in the chair when he reached out to caress my cheek with his hand.

"I do not think there is any swelling," he said as his fingertips gently traced a line from my earlobe to the side of my chin.

What are you doing? The words screamed inside my head, but were unheard to the outside world. He removed his hand as the waitress placed a cup of tea in front of me.

"A posto, grazie?" she asked, looking straight at me.

I returned her look with a bewildered stare of confusion.

Pierre spoke to save me. "A posto, grazie."

She smiled, nodded, and walked away.

"The waitress wanted to know if that was all," he said. "She must have assumed you spoke Italian. Sorry, my fault."

"Oh, I think she knew exactly what she was doing," I said.

"What do you mean?"

"Oh nothing." I did not feel like explaining the petty and bitchy nature women sometimes engaged in. It was obvious she wanted to embarrass me, probably because she was attracted to Pierre and it was a way for her to point out my inadequacies. "I did not know you spoke Italian?"

"Yes." After a moment, he continued, "Also Spanish and German." He spoke confidently, but not in a boastful way.

"And French too," I said.

He laughed. "Of course, it would be awkward if I could not speak my own language."

It was my turn to chuckle and I became aware of how relaxed I was in his company. It was like being with an old friend.

"Have you much work left to do in Ireland?" I asked, trying to move things along.

He shrugged before answering. "Not much. Maybe five or six weeks at most."

"How is Rebecca taking your impending departure?"

He took on a slight look of concern. His eye movements and the fact that he gently bit his lower lip told me it was not going to be an easy question for him to answer.

"She is your friend, isn't she?" he asked, his voice full of uncertainty.

"Yes, she is. But she hasn't said anything to me about you leaving. In fact, she seems to be putting on a show of indifference about it."

"I see," he said.

I wasn't sure if it was concern or surprise that he was thinking.

"You see, Pierre, she is my friend and I am worried she might get hurt."

"Ah, you are a good friend then." He spoke as he raised the cappuccino to his lips.

He was not telling me what I wanted to hear, or even what I did not want to hear. This vexed me a little, but I maintained my friendly manner and did not let my irritation show.

"Pierre, can I be honest with you?"

"Of course."

"I'm really worried about Rebecca."

"In what way?"

"She's changed these past few weeks. She's not as jovial as is her nature, and she seems to be withdrawing into herself."

"Oh, I see." He straightened his posture and leaned forward as he realised I was truly concerned. "I was not aware of this, but I have not known her very long and perhaps she...how would you say..." He paused, trying to think of the correct words. "Perhaps she presents a different face to you?"

"Perhaps. Does she seem sad in your company?" I asked.

"Mademoiselle! I would not be very nice if I let a woman be sad in my company, would I?"

"I'm serious, Pierre."

"So am I. We have a good time together. It's just..." He seemed reluctant to continue.

"Just what?"

"It's just that Rebecca comes across a bit too serious

about our relationship sometimes."

"How do you mean?"

"Well, she often talks or behaves like we are going to spend the rest of our lives together."

"Really?" I tried to appear neither surprised nor too well-informed about Rebecca's hopes.

"Anna, can I be honest with you?"

"Of course."

"I know you are her friend, but I would prefer if our conversation went no further than this table."

"I promise you, Pierre. You have my word." I felt uncomfortable to be put in a position where I might have to withhold information from my friend, but it was obvious it was the only way he was going to open up to me.

"Thank you." There was something like a look of relief in his expression. "Please do not misunderstand me, I do like Rebecca, but—"

"But what?" I asked, encouraging him to continue.

"It's just that we are very different people. How would you say...cheese and chalk?"

"Chalk and cheese," I corrected him.

He looked confused as he wondered what the difference was.

"Never mind," I said, smiling.

He smiled back at me, realising it would probably be too complicated for me to explain.

"But you seem to get on so well together," I said, getting back to the seriousness of our conversation.

"We do, but I've always made it clear I would be in Ireland for only a short time." He paused for a moment, showing a look of frustration at the situation with Rebecca. "From the start, Rebecca has been very intense, practically making plans for our future. I swear to you, Anna, I've never given her any reason to think our friendship was anything more than a causal relationship." He must have sensed my doubt, because he said, "Anna, I am not the type of man to mislead or lie to get my way with a woman."

He sounded and looked so genuine, I couldn't disbelieve him, even though, deep down, I desperately wanted to.

"You do realise, Pierre, girls usually look on a relationship a little differently from a man?"

"Yes, of course. I know that. But like I said, I am not a

man to lead a girl on. Rebecca made it quite clear she wanted to see me outside of her workplace, the hotel. I agreed, and why wouldn't I? She is very attractive, isn't she?"

I blushed, but I'm not sure why I did.

"So, I asked her out. But from the very beginning, I made it clear I would be leaving Ireland soon. Although I have told her, she does not seem to take it in."

There was honesty in his face. His eyes widened, almost as if they were pleading to be believed.

"When are you going out again?" I asked.

"I'm flying to Paris tonight. I will be back in five or six days. We have no plans until I return. Will you talk to her when I am gone?"

"Yes, I will."

"You are a good friend to her. I can see that. She is lucky to have you."

I smiled. It was not often I received compliments of any nature.

"I had better be going." I looked at my watch.

"Are you going back toward the hotel? Perhaps we could walk together."

"No, I'm going the other way. The bus stop is around the corner." I looked to indicate the direction.

"A pity," he said.

I had lied again for the umpteenth time that day. I knew it would have been nice to walk back through the city with him. To stop at windows and discuss the items displayed there—the flamboyant brushstrokes of a colourful landscape, or the intricate carving around the edges of an antique writing table. So often I had marvelled at such things while alone, with nobody to discuss and share my thoughts.

Eighteen

There was no reply from Rebecca's bell. I assumed it was working. The only indication at the front door was the already dim light in the switch flickering and going out as I pushed the grubby button in. A sixth sense, a gut feeling maybe, told me she was there and not answering. I kept looking for her familiar face to look out the top window, but she did not appear. All I could see were raindrops floating down, only visible when they entered the range of the tawny glow of the streetlamp. I was about to walk away when the door opened. The young couple that lived on the floor below her shuffled out, their gaunt eyes fixed rigidly on the ground as if in fear that eye contact would force them to acknowledge my presence. I slipped into the hall as they walked away without looking back. Their thin silhouettes faded into the night like ghostly apparitions disappearing before one's eyes.

I knocked and called her name, but there was no reply. Beneath the door, a dull flickering light that could only have been created by flames dancing in the fireplace shimmered back and forth across the faded landing carpet.

"Rebecca? Are you in there? It's me, Anna."

Silence answered me, a false silence that reeked of rejection. I pressed my ear against the door, listening for sound, any sound that would confirm her presence behind the locked door. I could not hear anything, but then, just for a moment, I thought I heard sobbing. It was subdued weeping, the sort of sobs that are muffled by a hanky and keep the pitiful cries subjective and not for the ears of the world. I continued to listen, my ear starting to hurt, such was the pressure of my head against the wood panelling of the door.

"Rebecca?" I called out, and knocked again, this time harder and with a renewed sense of urgency.

There was still no answer, and the stifled sniffling ceased, leaving me wondering if I had imagined it, letting the wind outside trick me, playing with my susceptible mind. I left with a feeling of emptiness, as if I had left part of me behind.

Three days passed and Rebecca did not go to work. When she did finally show on the fourth day, I was struck by her appearance. She looked tired, and walked as if weary from carrying a great weight upon her shoulders. Her smile, when she did smile, lacked conviction, and the usually natural and simple act seemed to come to her with great difficulty. She told me she had been unwell. Nothing serious, a stomach bug, that's all. I said nothing about the night I stood calling her name and banging on her door. The passing of time seemed to make the incident more difficult to discuss, and I suspected she would not have told me the truth anyway.

Our friendship stood, but something tangible hung over our rapport, like a dark cloud that promised rain but held back its deluge, knowing the threat of the cloudburst would be more worrisome than the impending rainfall.

Rodrigo, a man who seemed to treat life as if every day was a gift from God, took one look at her sad face and said, "Oh my lovely, Rebecca, cheer up for it may never happen, and if it does...well, what the hell!"

She laughed and it pleased Rodrigo. But I perceived labour in her laugh. It was brought forth with effort, the effort to please, the determination to fool, and the desperation to hide behind it.

More and more I found myself in the Drumcondra area. I wandered the narrow paths of Tolka Park, pausing to watch the flowing water run over the weir and cascade down into a swirling mayhem, boiling in white foam. Old women walked small dogs and here and there; young men walked large dogs straining at their leashes, eager to run free and rid themselves of the restricting leads. Without realising, or perhaps I did, I found myself on Hollybank Road and looking at the wine-coloured door of number one.

"Mr Cleary?" My voice was breaking nervously as I said his name. What finally possessed me to knock on his door, I did not know. I wasn't sure whether it was courage or a desperate longing that moved my feet up the three steps.

"Yes?" There was hesitancy in his voice. It was a reluctance I could understand. A stranger knowing one's name always left a person feeling at a disadvantage.

"You don't... I'm sorry... I'm so sorry." My courage waned. I could barely speak and my words crumbled like stale biscuits between squeezing fingers. I turned to leave, wishing the ground would open and swallow me up there and then.

"No wait!" His voice was low and polite, but it had authority. Like a teacher's voice, his words demanded obedience.

I stopped and turned back, but stood without speaking, not knowing what to say.

"You know my name?"

"Yes," I said, sounding like a scared mouse.

"Then, you came to see me?"

"Yes, I did."

He looked at me, waiting for me to state my business. I was overcome with a massive feeling of fear, emotion, and a sickening excitement that was overwhelmed with apprehension. It was the sort of apprehension a skydiver might experience as he looked out the open door of an aeroplane. Yes, he had a parachute, no, he wasn't going to die, but yet, his brain screamed, releasing stimulants into the bloodstream, making his heart pound furiously against his ribcage.

Finally, I managed to speak. "You don't know me, but I think you knew my mother," I finally said, the words coming from God knows where.

"Your mother?" His look of bewilderment showed he had no idea what was coming. I was about to hit him with a baseball bat. Either that, or I was about to make a complete fool of myself.

"Yes, Maria Matthews."

He continued to hold the same unchanging expression. The name seemed to mean nothing to him. I guessed it wasn't that he would have forgotten her and it was a case that the name coming out of the blue like it was meant his mind hadn't made the connection yet.

"Maria Matthews?" He looked at me as if I was crazy.

And then it dawned on me—Matthews was her married name. "O'Brien...I'm sorry, I meant Maria O'Brien."

Again, there was a look of bewilderment. Then something clicked into place as his mind struggled to put the pieces together.

"Maria?" His face drained of all colour and, for a moment, I thought he was going to faint. "You knew Maria?" His voice had weakened and there was a noticeable tremble as he spoke.

"Is there somewhere we can talk?" I asked, feeling awkward having the conversation on the doorstep.

"Yes, of course. But not here." He looked nervously over his shoulder. There was no one there, but the kitchen door was slightly ajar and I could hear noises coming from behind it—cutlery being moved, a cupboard closing. He looked back at me. "Do you know the coffee shop on the main road?" he asked, poking his head out the door and looking to the left and in the general direction of the local shops.

"Yes, I think so. Beside the minimarket?"

"Yes, that's the one. I'll meet you there in fifteen minutes, okay?"

I agreed and left. He closed the door and I could see some relief in his face that I was leaving, but also something else. It was that tentative anticipation about what he was going to hear in the cafe. I could see he had absolutely no idea whatsoever about who I was.

In the short time we talked at his door, I had studied him closely, looking for something familiar, some resemblance that would be obvious. I needed to know the truth. I needed to know who I was and where I'd come from. I wanted nothing from him other than that, the truth, whatever it was. I felt like a person with a piece missing. I was incomplete. But in those forty-five seconds, I had seen nothing. No resemblance to my own features. Our eyes were a different colour. His nose was strong and prominent, whereas mine was small and compact. His hair was dark. Mine was fair. He was tall, I was not. I saw nothing and it confused me. There was nothing that would reinforce my belief and give credence to my expectations. As I walked to the cafe, I convinced myself I had made a mistake. He could not be my father, he just could not be.

I waited in the coffee shop, having resisted the urge to walk home and forget what I was coming to believe to be a false pursuit. It was true he recognized my mother's name, but if he was my real father, surely I would have sensed something. But I felt nothing, nothing other than the cold exchange of words between strangers.

I found a table at the back wall and sat waiting, almost hidden from view by the other customers. Whatever Mr Cleary's relationship was with my mother, his look of fear left me in no doubt he would not want to sit at the window during our forthcoming conversation. Whatever his secret was, I suspected he would prefer to discuss it in the dark shadows where he would hope to have it remain.

I played with words, toyed with phrases, constructed sentences in my head. I thought about what I was going to say, how I was going to say it. I was nervous but, strangely enough, I wasn't lacking confidence. For once in my life, I was standing up and demanding to know who I was.

I knew what I wanted from him. I wanted the truth. What happened eighteen years ago? I needed to know. I had a right to know. I felt without that knowledge, I would always feel incomplete. I'd forever be alone, like a tree deep in the woods where no one could hear its branches creaking in the wind or the patter of raindrops hitting its leaves. If someone could see me, I'd know I was real, that I came from somewhere, and ultimately, who I was.

The cafe was busy. Women with shopping bags by their seats chatted and laughed and looked unburdened by life's woes. Cheeriness came easy, and it was second nature to them to smile, to laugh, to share their day with friends. I envied them, but wondered if I was deluding myself. Perhaps behind the happy faces were troubles and miseries that were hidden to the outside world.

I saw him pass the window, struggling to peer in through the glass that was blanketed in a foggy hue. It was only when he entered that he saw me hidden away behind the headscarves and nodding heads. He raised his head in recognition and I did the same. He did not smile. He did not frown. His expression was a neutral look, the type one shows an official behind a counter. A smile was not warranted because there was no friendship, and a frown was ill-advised as the person facing you may well have to ability to make things more difficult than they already were.

"I'm sorry about before," he said, pulling off his coat and draping it across the back of the chair. "I couldn't talk earlier." He pulled his scarf from around his neck, folding it neatly before laying it on the table.

"I understand," I said in a bland tone.

"No," he replied. His face took on a look of great seriousness. "I don't think you do understand. I don't think you have any idea whatsoever."

Nineteen

We sat facing each other, mirroring each other's discomfort. It was the type of unease one would experience when facing an interviewer for a job vacancy. You wait in anticipation, expecting to be quizzed on aspects of your life that, outside of the room, the person would never consider asking about. Neither of us knew what exactly was going to be discussed, what questions asked, what memories evoked, or what secrets uncovered.

He ordered coffee with a mere nod and the waitress returned his signal with a similar gesture. He was obviously a regular customer and the familiarity between the two boosted my feeling of self-worth by a small degree. By bringing me here, he wasn't afraid or embarrassed to be seen with me. It helped rid the feeling that I was a skeleton in his cupboard.

"Like I said" —he talked while fiddling with the saltcellar—"I'm sorry about before. It's just that you took me by surprise."

"I'm sorry. Maybe I should have phoned first?" It was a silly question, but I did not know how to go about asking him the one question that was burning away inside of me—*Are you my father?*

"No, that's okay," he said, sounding like he meant it, but I kept thinking back to his uncomfortable look when I appeared on his doorstep.

The girl arrived with his coffee, placed the mug down, and gave a common enough smile before turning on her heels to attend another table. He tasted the coffee and smiled with satisfaction as if confirming it was the taste he had become accustomed to at this particular cafe. He put the mug down and there was another uncomfortable silence as we both seemed to be waiting for the other to start.

"Why are you asking me about Maria?" he finally said.

I took a deep breath, finding it hard to believe I was about to have this conversation. It seemed so unreal, almost inconceivable, like a chapter from some trashy novel that one purchased simply to while away the tedious hours of a bus journey.

"Mr Cleary, I'm not sure how to say this—"

"Say what?"

"I could be completely mistaken, but..." Again, my voice broke, my words dissolving before they left my lips.

"What is your name?" he asked, realising my mind was in turmoil and helping by changing the subject.

"Anna. My name is Anna," I answered with a stupid feeling of relief. Relief that I was faced with such a simple question that I could answer without sounding like a babbling idiot. Relief as well that there was a respite from the topic I wanted to discuss, which when I think about it, made no sense at all.

"Well, Anna, it's nice to meet you." He smiled and raised his mug to toast our meeting.

I smiled back. I felt my cheeks glowing, but although embarrassed, I relaxed a little, put at ease by his display of friendliness.

"You asked me about Maria?" He did not say her second name, and it showed a close familiarity with her, as if he still knew her and she had just popped out on an errand.

"Yes. Maria was my mother."

His eyes widened, not in shock, but more in enlightenment.

"That answers something that has been bothering me," he said.

"What do you mean?"

"When I opened the door and saw you standing there, it was as if I knew you somehow, but just couldn't quite put my finger on it." His expression changed to a more sombre one. "I heard about Maria's death. I'm so sorry." He reached out and tenderly patted my hand.

"Thank you."

"But why have you come to see me?"

"Because I need you to answer a question."

"Which is?"

I could see in his face he had not the slightest inkling that I might be his daughter. He waited for me to continue while he took sips from the mug of coffee.

"My grandma told me you were my father."

There, I finally said it. A strange feeling of relief enveloped me. It was as if the question itself had been a millstone around my neck. Now it was gone. Whatever his reply, his reaction, his lies, his shame or embarrassment, it did not matter. I had freed myself of the heavy question that had weighed upon me.

His immediate response was one of slow shock. His eyes broadened and seemed to lose the power of being able to blink. They stared at me in disbelief, wide and transfixed. Colour drained from his face and his arm seemed to rapidly lose strength as he struggled to put down the mug before it fell from his grasp.

"Your grandmother...she said what?" His voice changed, the confident tone weakening as if his body was reverting back to that of a schoolboy and not a teacher.

"She said you were my father."

"But why? I don't understand."

"She said you were my mother's English teacher and that you had a relationship with her."

"No...I mean yes, but..."

Surprise had rendered him practically speechless, and I actually felt sorry for him, which was something I had not expected. I watched as he slowly shook his head in disbelief, trying to grasp the enormity of my statement. He leaned back in the chair as if a great invisible force was pushing against his chest. Why was I sympathising with him? The question intrigued me. Despite any preconceptions I held before our meeting, I discovered I actually liked Robert Cleary. He had a pleasant air about him and, despite having just met, I could sense a genuine side to his character that was not anticipated. For some reason, had it not been for the topic under discussion, I would have felt quite comfortable in his company. It took a few minutes for him to compose himself and start to think clearly about what he wanted to say.

"What age are you, Anna?"

"I was eighteen last month."

He leaned back, deep in thought.

"And you are Maria O'Brien's daughter?"

"Yes."

"I don't understand...it just doesn't make sense." He shook his head again in disbelief.

"What doesn't?" I said.

"Is it possible?" he said, looking at me, but asking himself the question.

"What do you mean?" I asked.

"It is true we had a relationship, but..." He stopped mid-sentence, lost in thought as if trying to mentally slot scraps of information into place. "Anna, tell me exactly what your grandmother told you...please, it's important."

He listened in polite silence, with an expression of intense concentration as I told him everything I knew. The din of the cafe ebbed into the background and, for those few minutes, we became the only two people there as the whole world faded into obscurity.

A short while later, we found ourselves walking along the pebbled paths of Tolka Park. We had left the coffee shop after the seriousness of our talk seemed to make the indoor surroundings oppressive and claustrophobic. The fresh air was like medicine to a troubled mind, leaving us to better absorb the facts and think more clearly about what we were saying.

It was dark when I got home. Grandpa and Peter had been fighting again. Nobody told me of their argument, no one had to. The unfriendly atmosphere hung heavily like a great cloud of unhappiness. Peter had retreated to the safety of his room, losing his troubled thoughts in the pounding throb of music coming out of his beloved radio. Grandpa sat stoking the burning coals of the fire, prodding the embers so they sparked and hissed in the confines of the fireplace.

I sat with Grandma in the kitchen. She looked older than usual, her face weary from life. I watched her thin fingers etched with veins clasp themselves around a bowel of turnip soup, absorbing the heat as if it was a life preserving source.

"Did you have a good day, Anna?" she asked, her voice sounding weak and tired.

"Yes, Grandma," I said, concealing the truth about meeting my father. I did not think she would be angry with me. That was something I could never imagine, but she seemed so tired, I thought it best not to unload my news onto her worn-out shoulders.

"Have you eaten?" she asked.

"Yes, Grandma, I had dinner at the hotel." I lied again. There was nothing cooked and the stove was piled high with dirty pots and unwashed plates. I knew that despite her exhaustion, she would have jumped to her feet and made me a dinner while trying to appear happy about doing it. "You look tired."

"Yes, Anna, I feel very tired lately."

"You do too much, Grandma. All the cooking and cleaning, and your job at the laundrette as well."

She shrugged.

"I could do the cooking for you, if you want. It would be one less thing for you to do."

She shook her head defiantly. It was a reaction that did not surprise me. Grandma was old-fashioned in her ways. She felt it was her job to run the house, and allocating a task to someone else would be an admission of failure in her mind.

Any more offers of help I made were greeted with a similar refusal. I gave up, realising my efforts were pointless. I watched her prepare for bed, her face seeming older and more worn-out, her weary body exerting itself as she made her way up the stairs.

Twenty

Life began to feel better. And indeed it was. It was like going to bed listening to the rain driven against the window by a howling gale and waking to find the sky clear— the sun's warmth reaching down, rejuvenating and forgiving and washing away the previous day's sins.

After eighteen years, I had met my father. While I'd only recently learned of his existence, the news had been so overwhelming, I felt as if I'd hardly lived at all. I was not a complete person and without knowing the truth, I truly believed I would have gone through life unable to rid myself of that feeling. There would have been an empty space inside me—a void demanding answers to fill it. Without those answers, the void would have remained and maybe even grown to consume me in self-doubt and unhappiness.

As if meeting Robert Cleary had not lifted my spirits, more good news greeted me when I came home from work. Grandpa had gone to visit his brother in Athlone. He would be away for a week, Grandma told me. Perhaps it was because of some sense of expected loyalty, but whatever the reason, she told me without any sign of emotion. She did not smile or even frown. It was a neutral look reserved for the passing of information, nothing more and nothing less. However, a joy was obvious in her actions. She hummed cheery tunes as she went about her business. The house seemed to brighten without his suffocating presence. Potted plants appeared on the parlour's window sill, their crimson and blue petals causing the little terraced house to stand out against the other homes along the street. The placing of flower pots seemed to have an infectious effect on the neighbours, because two days later, a colourful bouquet of chrysanthemums appeared in the window of another house across the street. The following day, another householder adopted the same idea and so it continued until nearly two dozen window ledges came alive with colourful arrays of floral arrangements.

But the happiness of seventy-six Ignatius Road did not spread to the hotel. Rebecca became more distant and, although not unfriendly, she seemed absorbed in problems she did not want to share with anyone else. She did not come to work on Tuesday or Wednesday. Mr Wilkinson, the hotel manager, asked me If I knew why she was absent as she neglected to inform them of any illness. He was pleasant, but I could sense an underlying anger and I suspected her job could be in jeopardy. I decided to call on her that night.

Oh Rebecca, poor Rebecca. She looked like a train wreck, broken and twisted. Her dishevelled pyjamas matched her dejected state. I tried not to look shocked, but it would have been impossible to conceal my concern. Even if I could not hide my distress for her, Rebecca seemed incapable of taking in anything outside of her own personal torments.

"When did you last eat?" I asked, noticing the empty cupboard above the sink that was crammed with filthy dishes.

"This morning...or maybe last night." She shrugged with the indifference of someone that had given up on life.

"Is there anything at all?" I said, rummaging around the chaos of the kitchen units.

She didn't answer, and when I looked around, she was sitting on the edge of the bed staring at the opposite wall as if mesmerized by the faded wallpaper pattern that repeated itself from top to bottom and side to side. I was determined to find out what ailed her, what crippling problem it was that had taken such a firm grasp and zapped the life out of her like water wrung from a wet dishcloth. Before I could delve into her mind, there was work to be done. I cleaned the room, scraped dried food from plates, and built a fire with the last heap of coal. I took her keys and walked to the corner shop. Half an hour later, I watched as she played with the food on her plate, only occasionally lifting the fork to her mouth.

"What's wrong?" I finally asked in a solemn voice.

"Nothing, it's fine."

"Not the food, Rebecca, I mean what's really wrong?"

She looked at me for a moment, her eyes heavy with the weight of sadness. Then she looked away as if embarrassed.

I sat beside her, putting my arm around her shoulders.

"For heaven's sake, Rebecca, I know something is troubling you. What is it? You can tell me. I am your friend after all, aren't I?"

She stared at me and I feared how she might answer my question.

"Anna...you are my friend. You are my best friend, and I have treated you badly."

"No you haven't," I said.

"Yes I have. I got so wrapped up with Pierre that I neglected our friendship. I took you for granted, and for that I'm sorry."

"You have nothing to be sorry about." I tightened my grasp around her shoulders, sensing she was on the verge of opening up. I felt her tremble, and it was as if opening up might mean cracking up.

"Anna..." Her voice trailed off in a tremble. Her bottom lip began to quiver, and I suddenly became more worried. She tried to speak, but no words came out. She started to whimper, low like a baby's cry before it fully wakes. The sob grew louder until it became an uncontrollable whine that seemed to echo the total accumulation of all human wretchedness before channelling it through the lungs of one misfortunate. Rebecca fell across my lap, her body jerking in harmony with every pitiful sob.

I held her, stroking her head like one might caress a cat. I did not speak, but hushed gently while tears flowed freely and without abate from her burdened eyes.

The fire's flames that had leapt and danced with such gusto slowly but surely weakened, withdrawing downward, each to the blackened lump of coal that had been its origin. The room gradually darkened as the flickering shadows crept back along the walls toward the fireplace. Rebecca's crying finally stopped and she lay quietly, still in the same position with only the gentle noise of her breathing to be heard.

I fell asleep. It wasn't for long, but when I woke, Rebecca was up and making tea. The kettle had just boiled and greyish plumes of steam billowed up and lingered, trapped under the wall press above it.

"Tea?" she asked.

"Yes...thank you."

"I got some sticks for the fire," she said, moving her arm with the gesture of a half wave toward the fireplace.

"How do you feel?" I asked, hoping she would not lie. Her eyes were still red, almost looking as if they were swollen.

"Not good," she said, looking as if the tears might come again at any moment.

"Rebecca, you have to tell me what's wrong. You have to let me help you."

"I don't think anyone can help me now."

"Why would you say such a thing?"

"Because it's true." Her face hardened in its expression.

"Stop it, please, you're frightening me," I said. "What can be so bad?"

She put her cup down and looked at me with a mixture of sadness and hopelessness.

"I'm pregnant," she sobbed.

I did not say anything. A state of utter shock made me freeze in position, like one of those old Greek statues that had trapped the model's stance for all of eternity to come.

"Well, say something," she said.

I tried to answer, but it took a few moments before I had control of my functions again. My throat had gone so dry it seemed to snare my words before they could escape.

"You're pregnant?" I finally blurted out.

She nodded, pursing her lips together.

"Does Pierre know?"

She nodded again.

"And what has he said about it?"

"He's not happy."

"No, I can see why he wouldn't be."

In that brief moment, my heart went out to Rebecca. Her confident look had vanished. She resembled a lost child, her expression displaying all the signs of fear, loneliness, and despair.

"How long have you known?" I asked.

"A few weeks."

"I know you said Pierre was not happy, but surely you are discussing the situation with him?"

"Not really, we are not talking at the moment."

"But that's ridiculous. The two of you have a lot to talk about."

She shrugged and went to sit by the fire.

I sat beside her and felt the dying heat of the wood warm my face. There was no more talk on the subject that night. It had taken a lot out of Rebecca to confide in me, and I sensed she wanted to leave it at that for the moment.

We sat together as the fire dwindled. Exhaustion overcame her and she fell asleep on the bed without undressing. Even asleep, her face was troubled. She looked as if she had aged ten years in just a few weeks. I covered her with a blanket, stroked her hair for a moment as I told her everything would be alright. I knew she could not hear me, but I hoped my words might find a way into her subconscious mind and help to ease her troubled dreams.

Twenty-One

I longed to tell someone about Robert Cleary. Rebecca was the only one I could confide in, but it seemed wrong to exclaim my joy while she was consumed with despair. Good news was meant to be spread, to be shared with those close to the heart. The concealment of joy seemed so unnatural I wondered if it truly existed if no one else knew. But I discounted that question the moment I thought it, for my heart abounded with happiness.

I wanted to tell her about our first meeting and how we talked for a whole afternoon. And how, contradictory to any preconceived expectations, there was no loathing in my heart, no burning desire to condemn or berate. I found no hatred, felt no repulsion, and lacked any harbouring of ill feelings toward him. Those feelings, if they were present, never materialized. Not after he opened up to me as we strolled between the flower beds in Tolka Park.

He cried. He actually cried. I'd never seen a grown man weep before, other than those I observed at funerals. It wasn't a flood of tears, or even a trickle. I thought I saw one tear about to run over his eyelid just before he wiped away the evidence. But his eyes had reddened. They had that melancholy look one would often have at the end of a sad story. He did not look pitiful or weak. If anything, it endeared me more to him. It was impossible to hate him, not after he told me what had happened all those years ago.

"I didn't know," he had said. "I truly didn't know."

I had found that hard to believe at first. How could he not

have known? It didn't make sense. Then he told me how he had called at seventy-six Ignatius Road. He didn't know what he was going to say when the door opened. What could he possibly say to the parents of a girl he had impregnated? Not just any girl, but one of his seventeen-year-old students. The only thing he knew for certain was that he wasn't going to shirk his responsibilities or hide behind a wall of denials. But then he learned the truth. Or at least what he believed to be the truth.

Grandpa had opened the door. He was alone in the house and Robert could not remember where he was told Grandma was that evening.

"There is no baby," Grandpa had said to him.

Robert was taken aback in confusion, although flabbergasted was the word he used when telling me.

"What do you mean no baby?" he asked, his voice almost breaking as he spoke.

"Maria had a miscarriage. The baby died," Grandpa said, his face showing no emotion, his eyes cold and his lips unnaturally straight, as Robert had described him.

"A miscarriage...when?"

"Three days ago."

"And where is she now?" Robert asked, longing to see her, to comfort her, to rock her in his arms and tell her everything would be all right.

"She's gone."

"Gone where?"

"England. She wanted to get away from here, from everyone that knew her, and away from you."

"But—"

Robert tried to protest, but Grandpa interrupted him, anger seemingly growing inside of him. "Now you listen to me, Robert Cleary. All it will take is one phone call and you will lose your job. I'll see to it that you never teach again."

"I'm not trying to conceal anything, Mr O'Brien. On the contrary, I'm quite prepared to give up teaching so we can be together. To make things right for Maria."

"Well, you're wasting your time if you think Maria wants anything to do with you."

"I can't believe that," Robert protested.

"Grow up, man!" Grandpa shouted. "Do you think you were the only one?"

"What do you mean?" Robert asked.

"Do you think you were the only man Maria opened her legs for?"

Robert was stunned into silence. He didn't believe what he was hearing and was shocked that a man could talk in such a derogatory fashion about his own daughter.

"The fact is," Grandpa said, "she has no idea who the father was. As far as we can make out, it could have been one of half a dozen men."

Robert's shocked moment of silence continued, his mind a maelstrom of confusion. Nothing Grandpa said seemed to fit Maria's character as he knew it. Could he have been so blind? If it had been anyone else saying those things, he would have denounced them as an outright liar and probably would have punched them on the nose, although, he did confess to never having punched anyone in his entire life. But the fact that it was Maria's father telling him those dreadful things made him discount them without putting any thought into the fact that it might be a tissue of lies. What did occur to him was that he was getting an insight into Grandpa's character. What father would openly say such filthy things about his daughter, whether they were true or not? He despised my grandpa there and then, but despite his revulsion for the man, he walked away with the mistaken belief he had been told the truth.

"I can never forgive myself," he said, his eyes begging my understanding if not my forgiveness. "I should never have believed those horrible lies."

We sat on a small wall and watched the water flowing toward the weir. There was something therapeutic about moving water. I remembered sitting once on the rocks overlooking Sligo bay, and for hours I was mesmerised by the waves rolling toward me. They seemed gentle and slow moving in the distance, but then quickened and grew as they washed up onto the shore. Each wave seemed to erode away at my fears little by little as the incoming tide worked its way along the golden sand. It was the same feeling I experienced as I watched the grey canal water flow past. Between the lock gates, the water was still, almost stagnant, but close to the weir. It surged forward to tumble over the small drop. There it swirled and bubbled in a melee of white foam. It was similar to a mini waterfall, but there was no roar of cascading water, the shallow drop only resulting in a low, gentle, and constant drone.

There was a long silence as we sat, hypnotized by the calming noise of flowing water that soothed our thoughts and massaged our worries until they seemed small and almost insignificant.

Robert was the first to break the silence. "Anna, I can't forgive myself and I wouldn't ask you to forgive me either, but if you understood, I think it might help the both of us."

I didn't answer straight away. I knew what I was going to say, but it seemed appropriative to think about the question, much like a jury after the judge sends them out to deliberate. It just wouldn't do for them to return too soon. The judge, the lawyers, and probably the defendant alike, would be disheartened at their refusal to discuss, to argue, or even dwell on the complexities of the case. Whatever the verdict, there would be someone aggrieved at their neglect of duty.

So I waited, attempting to transport myself, mentally speaking, back to that evening when Grandpa opened the door to him. It didn't require much imagination to picture Grandpa's harsh expression and the permanent glower he was never without. I could clearly hear his abrupt and cruel voice dictating the conversation. After a suitable length of time had passed, which I had deemed around one minute appropriate, I answered him.

"Robert—" It seemed strange to address him as anything else. I could hardly call him Dad, and Mr Cleary would be ridiculously formal considering he was my father. "I'm not really sure why I came to see you. I mean, there's nothing I want from you, not anything that I could explain anyway."

"But something made you knock on my door?"

"Yes, you're right, something did. Have you ever..." I paused, trying to construct an example in my head. He said nothing and waited for me to continue. There was a look of interest in his expression, like he really put value on every word I spoke. "I know this is going to sound silly, but—"

"Go on," he said in an encouraging tone.

"Have you ever held your hand over a flame, maybe a candle for instance, just to see what happens?"

"I don't follow," he said, and I began to feel a little foolish.

"What I'm trying to say is, you shouldn't do it. You know it's wrong, stupid even, but a compelling urge overrides all your sensible thinking."

"Are you saying it was wrong to contact me?"

"No, not now that I've done it, and I'm glad I did. But before, when I stood outside your house, I was convinced no good could come of it. Yet, something I cannot explain made me walk up those steps and knock on the door. I don't remember what I was thinking. To be honest, I'm not sure if I *was thinking.*"

"I'm glad you did." He reached out and gently squeezed my arm. There was something reassuring about his touch. It wasn't the touch of a stranger, the type that induced an instant recoil. There was something instinctively right about it, and I wondered if I had not known who he was, would I have still have felt the same safe sensation?

"I wasn't intending to embarrass or cause you any trouble," I said.

"What do you mean?"

"You seemed uncomfortable at the door. I'm guessing it was inconvenient for you to talk?" I was proud of myself for phrasing the question so delicately. I really wanted to find out if he was married. Did he have children, did I have a sibling? I was dying to know, and he had no idea how much.

"Oh...I see. No, you don't understand." His eyes widened in realisation as he read between the lines. "It's just that, Yvonne was there."

"Your wife?"

"Oh no, we're not married. She's my girlfriend. She's a lecturer at Belfast University. Sometimes she comes down to spend the weekend and I do the same. Going up to Belfast, I mean."

"What would she make of all this, I wonder?" I wondered if he was going to tell her, but it was more than just a question, it was a test. I figured if he was capable of concealing this from her, then it would reveal something about his character, something that would not endear me to him.

"I'll soon find out," he said, and chuckled.

"You are going to tell her?"

"Of course, as soon as I get home."

"What do you think she will say?"

"I don't know, but I think she will be okay with it."

"And if she's not?"

"Well, I'll cross that bridge when I come to it."

"I'm sorry. I didn't mean to cause you problems."

"You didn't cause anything, Anna. This is my own doing, but it's not a problem. It's just the way things have turned out. And do you know what?"

"What?"

"I'm glad. I'm glad you knocked on my door this morning."

"Really?"

"Yes, really."

He looked at me and I did not feel uncomfortable retuning the look. His eyes were a mixture of both joy and sadness, if that was possible.

We walked to the park gates and went our separate ways, but not before arranging to meet again in a few days' time. He leaned down and kissed me on the cheek, giving me a light hug as he did. It was a bit embarrassing for both of us, but after I left and walked along the Drumcondra Road, I was glad he showed me that sign of affection. It helped strengthen the bond between us from strangers to something more.

Twenty-Two

The warm and cheery atmosphere ended the moment Grandpa returned. My stomach had churned at the mere thought of him coming home. While nothing could now endear me to him, it was for Grandma's sake only that I hoped the short holiday would have mellowed him a little, even for just a few days to give her a respite from his horrible manner. But I was mistaken. When he pushed open the door and I saw his stern face glaring at me, an invisible cloud of harshness and detestation seemed to rush in with him like a cold blast of winter air. I received the characteristic grunt as he passed me in the hallway.

"Did you have a good time?" Grandma asked, as if he had only been gone a few hours.

He mumbled something in reply and accompanied it by raising his upper lip to blow a puff of breath upwards.

"How's your brother?" she asked, only to receive a similar reply.

That was the last mention of his trip to Athlone by anyone in the house and, within five minutes, it felt as if he'd never left at all.

Rebecca's downward fall into depression continued and my attempts to cheer her up had little, if any, affect. She returned to work and simply went through the motions of her daily routine without any enthusiasm or liveliness. After two days, she disappeared again much to the annoyance of the management.

Then Pierre returned. I had not known of his arrival and got a shock when I saw him standing at the reception desk signing the register. I had to talk to him. What would come of it, I did not know, but Rebecca needed help and perhaps Pierre might succeed where I had failed.

Petra agreed to cover my absence should anyone ask for me. I changed out of my uniform in the toilet and slipped out the side door. I hoped Pierre would leave for his customary stroll around midday. I intended to talk to him when he got out of sight from the hotel.

At midday, just as the protruding clock from Cleary's department store struck twelve, he came out the door and turned toward the river. I hurried across the road, receiving an angry roar from a driver as I dodged through the traffic.

"Pierre!" I called out, barely able to keep up with him as he marched forward as if with a purpose.

He didn't hear me because of the rumble from buses and cars. I was closer when I called out a second time. He looked around and saw me puffing and panting as I approached him.

"Anna?" He was surprised and looked embarrassed, as if caught unawares.

"I need to talk to you," I said, struggling to regain my breath.

"About what?" he asked, but it was obvious he knew what I wanted to discuss.

"About Rebecca," I said, and seeing the dispassionate expression he showed, I added, "And the baby."

He nodded, slow and unenthusiastically.

"Damn it, Pierre, this is important. We have to talk." I rarely if ever lost my temper, but the desperation of Rebecca's situation was bringing my anger to the surface like a pot of water on a slow boil.

He nodded, this time with acceptance that we did indeed have to talk. "Come, Anna." He pointed across the road to Cleary's. "I will buy you coffee."

The warmth of the store was welcoming after coming in from the cold. Soft music played throughout the shop, and we made our way to the cafe on the top floor.

He sat looking uncomfortable and no more wanting to

discuss the subject than he would want to have a tooth pulled.

"Rebecca told me everything," I said.

"Everything?"

"Yes," I replied.

He sipped from his coffee cup, looking at me warily as if doubting what I had said. His questionable glance confused me, because I already mentioned I knew about the baby.

"Anna," he said, carefully centering his cup on its saucer. "I know you are a good friend to Rebecca and please do not take what I say as rude, because I do not mean it in that vein." He paused for a moment as if wondering whether to continue. Then he took a short breath and said, "What has occurred between me and your friend is not really any concern of yours, is it?" He spoke almost apologetically, for fear he might show rudeness and, once again, I found him a hard man to dislike.

"It's Rebecca I'm worried about. She's very depressed."

"Depressed?" he asked, and I gathered from his expression he did not know what the word meant.

"It means she's very down, not going to work, not eating properly. Do I have to go on?"

"Ah, depression," he said, nodding.

"Depression?"

"Yes, it is French pronunciation for what you mean. But Rebecca and I are finished as far as a relationship goes, so I am not sure what you want from me."

"Don't you think it's a bit cruel?"

He looked at me as if he had no comprehension of what I was saying.

"For heaven's sake, Pierre. Don't you think you should shoulder some of the responsibility?"

"Well...no, why should I?"

I leaned back in the chair, amazed at his indifferent attitude. I don't think I'd ever been so annoyed, and it took all my self-control not to shout at him.

"Pierre, you can't simply turn your back on her. You can't just walk away like nothing has happened."

He put down his coffee and leaned forward as if to whisper. While not quite a whisper, he did talk in a lower voice. "What exactly has Rebecca told you?"

"Do you mean about the baby?"

"Yes, but what else?"

"Just that you're not happy about it and you have finished with her."

He leaned back again. "That's what she told you, just that?"

"Yes," I said.

"Anna..." He slowly shook his head. "There's a bit more to it than that."

"What do you mean?"

"I mean, Rebecca has been economical with the truth."

I didn't say anything. I wondered what he was getting at and suspected he was going to spin the details to suit himself.

"I told you before, Anna, I had made it clear to Rebecca that a long term relationship was not what I was looking for."

I nodded, but I didn't see what difference that made. Obviously, the pregnancy was unexpected and he should be prepared to alter his plans.

"But, Rebecca had different ideas," he said.

"What are you saying?"

"I'm saying she got pregnant on purpose." He watched my look of disbelief for a moment and then stared at me as if desperate to be believed. "I'm serious, Anna. She told me we didn't have to worry, that she had taken a pill, but she lied. She knew there was a good chance she would get pregnant." He paused for a moment, as if to let what he said sink in. "She knew exactly what she was doing."

I began to grow angry again. It was a slow rage building up deep inside me, getting itself to the right temperature before it rose to the surface. My body and mind were like a volcano about to explode. The strange thing was, I didn't know who to be angry with. Pierre was the obvious choice, but what if he was telling me the truth? If Rebecca had really planned and trapped him, then surely some if not all of my anger should be toward her. If that was the case, I wanted to be angry with myself for getting involved and making a fool of myself by having no idea of the facts.

Pierre must have had a good ability in perceiving people, because as if warned by a silent voice, he moved to prevent any outburst on my part.

"Anna." His voice was soft, and I cursed the calming effect it demanded of me. "I know you do not want to hear this. I realise it is not want you expected, but it is the truth."

I shook my head, unable or maybe unwilling to take in what he had told me.

"Rebecca set out to trap me by getting herself pregnant. I know this because she has admitted it to me."

"She told you that?"

"Yes, she did. She was furious when I told her we were finished. She claimed I could not walk away. She was like a woman possessed. Anna, I think you have not seen your friend like this before?"

I nodded and then shook my head in confusion, not knowing what to say. As much as I did not want to admit it, I knew there was a manipulative side to Rebecca, and perhaps there was some truth in what he was saying.

"I have to get back to work," I said, standing up and probably appearing a little flustered. I had come to see him with a definite purpose in mind, and that was to make him aware of his responsibilities. But I was leaving, not knowing what to think or what to do next.

"Will you meet me when you finish work?" He stood, as if his request might carry more weight by doing so.

"Why?"

"Because there is more I have not told you and as you want to help your friend, you may as well know everything."

"All right." I found myself agreeing without considering whether I wanted to or not.

We walked to the main door and went in separate directions. He strolled casually, looking in shop windows as if he hadn't a care in the world. I hurried away and back toward the hotel, hoping my absence was not missed. I entered through the rear of the kitchen and Rodrigo, seeing me out of uniform, put two and two together and guessed I had snuck out.

"You naughty girl," he said, waving a large wooden ladle in the air. I blushed and continued on to where I could change in the restroom. I could hear his hearty laugh as the doors swung shut behind me. I was not worried, knowing that Rodrigo would never say anything to get me into trouble.

Twenty-Three

I finished work at six o'clock, changed my clothes, and then made my way to Madigan's Bar on Abbey Street. I think Pierre had suggested we meet there because he liked the traditional atmosphere of the place. The pub had so far escaped the renovation craze sweeping across the city. Modernisation was the pet word of those seeking change, allowing architects a free hand to design faceless buildings that were springing up around the capital. The bland trend had also found its way into newly renovated pubs. Plastic and glass seemed to be the two materials most favoured by young designers fresh from college, eager to experiment and show their skills. Seating became almost nonexistent other than a smattering of bright-coloured stools lined up against bar counters that consisted mostly of glass. The old landscape paintings and dusty bookshelves were replaced by modern prints, usually black-and-white, and gaudy jukeboxes. But Madigan's retained its old-style feeling with its wooden floors, varnished counters, and differing sized tables spread around without any hint of uniformity.

I was early, or he was late. I wasn't sure, having forgotten my watch. A clock behind the bar looked as if it hadn't worked in years. The black hands stood out sharply against the white face and both were pointing at twelve. The lounge was quiet and dim, its one window made up with small squares of darkened green and red glass. It reminded me of a church leaded glass window, but instead of religious figures, the roughened panels displayed an image of the pub's name and an image of a pint of ale.

Feeling self-conscious, I bought lemonade and hid myself away at a table in the corner. The minutes ticked by, and although I had no watch, I knew by now he was late.

"What the hell am I doing here?" I mumbled to myself. Did I want to hear what he was going to say or did I even care? Was I really going to help Rebecca by hearing the gritty details of her liaisons with him? Then paranoia set in. Why exactly did he want to meet me? Was it really to explain things or did he have an ulterior motive? Maybe I was to be his next conquest. *Oh for heaven's sake, Anna. Grab hold of yourself!*

No doubt it was only about ten minutes, but if felt like I had been waiting hours. I finished my lemonade and stood to leave. As I pushed the main door open, I came face to face with Pierre. His face was flushed, like he'd hurried to get here. Despite his probable exertion, he still looked unstressed.

"Anna, I'm late. I know. My apologies, mademoiselle, it is unforgivable, but I was held up on the phone with our European manager. He has...what is it the Irish say...the gift of the gab?"

I couldn't help smiling. There was something humorous in hearing Irish sayings when said with a French accent. "It's okay, no problem," I said, desperately trying to sound casual and indifferent.

"You are too kind." He bowed apologetically. "I have a craving for an Irish coffee. Will you join me?"

I nodded, feeling guilty he had caught me leaving. We sat at a table in the middle of the lounge. His choice of seating interested me, although I doubt anyone else would have given it a second thought. Had I been let to choose, I would have picked a table at the back, hidden in the shadows. I reasoned it was something to do with confidence. Ask a hundred self-assured people to select a table and they would invariably sit in full view of everyone. Ask a hundred introverts, and the opposite would prevail.

"This is nice," he said, his voice disturbing my thoughts. "There is something soothing about pubs in Ireland when they're not busy, like now. There is an atmosphere that will not be found anywhere else."

"Yes, but you did not ask me here to talk about Irish pubs."

"No, no I didn't. Forgive me." A serious expression spread across his face.

There was something about his eyes when he apologised. They made me think of a small boy in trouble, scared and apprehensive at what might happen next. In contrast to his broad frame, his eyes seemed to weaken as if betraying a false image. It was an unusual trait and one hard to deny.

"We came to talk about Rebecca, to see if we can help her, yes?"

"Yes," I said warily. "But you said, *we*. I thought you had finished with her?"

"I have, in a way, but she *is* carrying my baby. What type of man would I be if I walked away completely?"

"I thought—"

"You thought," he said, raising a hand to interrupt me. "You thought I might run away from my responsibilities and wash my hands of the whole problem?"

"Well...yes," I said with uncertainty in my voice.

"No, I am not that man. Rebecca might have conspired to ensnare me, but there will be a baby, and he or she will not be to blame for any of this."

I was taken aback and felt guilty for not expecting gallantry on his part.

"Have you discussed this with her...what happens after the baby arrives, I mean?"

He threw his hands in the air. "I tried, but she refused to discuss it. Her attitude is either we are a couple...or we are not. There is no in between." He sat silently for a moment with a genuine look of frustration. "Has she spoken to you about this?"

"No," I said, pausing while I thought back to the conversation I had with Rebecca in her flat. "She only told me you were angry and the relationship was over. I just assumed you wanted nothing more to do with her or a baby."

"No, as I have said to you, that is not the man I am."

I did not notice the hours pass. We talked and talked, about Rebecca, about relationships and responsibilities, and finally about his home in France. The conversation had started to drift after we ordered a bottle of French wine. Pierre could not talk about the wine country without assuming a melancholy gaze. It was as if his heart was intertwined with the vineyards and mentioning it reminded him that he was not where he belonged. He spoke of his father's château as if it was a woman and she was a goddess to be worshiped, like a Greek deity that exuded beauty and splendour that entwined one's soul to those that are willing to open up their hearts to her.

"It really does sound like a beautiful place," I said.

"Oh, Anna, I swear to you, if you smelt the sweet scent in the air during harvesting, or laid eyes on a thousand vines carpeting the hillside, swaying in the warm summer breeze, then..." He paused. I think it was to let me absorb the scene. "Then you would understand."

I smiled. It was impossible not to. It was like listening to a poet, creating a poem from words just as an artist used pastels.

I'm not sure how much wine I drank. It wasn't much, three glasses I think. I wasn't drunk, a little merry maybe, but I did know what I was doing. The influence of alcohol could not be used as a mitigating factor for my following actions.

Pierre insisted on me getting a taxi home. I shunned the suggestion, insisting I'd walk, but he was adamant. He accompanied me to the taxi rank opposite the hotel. He paid the driver in advance while waving away my protests. He pulled the rear door open and stood, waiting for me to get in.

"Goodnight, Pierre," I said, and lingered for a second before attempting to move. Why I paused I can't explain, not logically anyway, for there was no logic in my thoughts. It was as if I was plummeting down a ski slope at terrific speed, with only a split-second to decide if I should fall over and try to slide to a stop, or shoot off the end of the ramp and rise into the air like a soaring eagle. It was that lack of clear thought that governed my movements.

He leaned down to kiss me on the cheek, but his movements seemed to have a deliberate slowness to them. I turned my face and his lips met mine. His breath was warm and smelt of red wine. It all happened slow and without urgency or awkwardness. When our lips did part, it was with the same act of deliberate slowness, as if to reinforce the intimacy of the moment.

"Goodnight, Anna."

I smiled and so did he. Neither of us showed any hint of embarrassment. There was something natural about what had happened. I felt it, and so did he.

The taxi drove through the darkened streets of Summerhill. Children still played outside the corporation flats, despite the darkness. They swung from ropes lashed around telephone poles, screaming in delight as friends pushed them. The driver chatted away, polite conversation he no doubt repeated to every passenger that rode in his car. But his words were distant as my mind was elsewhere. I felt as if I'd been kissed for the first time.

It was late when I got home and all was not well in number seventy-six. Grandpa was in a rage of sorts, finding fault in everyone and everything.

"You stupid woman!" His words lashed Grandma like a whip. She did not answer, knowing any reply would only antagonise him.

Listening to Grandpa's raised voice from the safety of my room, I realised the reason for his temper. Grandma had given Peter some of her shopping money. He was broke and had been hanging around the house for several days. She took pity on him and gave him enough money to buy a few drinks.

"Will you never learn, you stupid woman?" His voice thundered around the house, the venom in his tone coming through the floorboards and filling the house with his horrible temperament like a bad odour.

I thought I heard Grandma crying in her room a little later on. It was a low, heart-wrenching whimper. I desperately wanted to go to her, to comfort her, to be more than a granddaughter. I wanted to be her friend, to hold her hand and wipe her tears. But fear of seeing Grandpa's brutish face glaring at me kept me in my room, and I left her to sob quiet, unseen tears.

Twenty-Four

I was glad Pierre was not in the hotel the next day. He'd flown out early and would not be back for two days. I did not want to see him, and yet, I did, all in the same mixed-up thought that was one of the many contradictions swimming around my head.

"Anna." The receptionist called out to me.

"Yes?" I answered, expecting another chore.

"Mr Wilson wants to see you in his office."

"Now?" I asked, horrified at the thought of being summoned to the manager's office.

"He's free now if you want to go up."

I nodded, but I did not want to go. It could only be bad news for me, and my mind fell into panic wondering what that reason might be.

My feet dragged as I made my way there. I stood outside the door, listening to his muffled voice as he spoke on the phone. I resigned myself to the thought that he knew about my absence yesterday. How he found out, I wasn't sure. Rodrigo would have never breathed a word, of that I was certain. Had Petra informed on me? She had promised to cover for me and although I didn't know her very well, I could not imagine her telling. Unless, of course, she had been put on the spot and may have had to tell the truth rather than find herself in trouble.

I heard him finish his call and I tapped gently on the door, so gently he might not hear and I could walk away, hoping to be forgotten about.

"Come in."

"You wanted to see me?" I stood half in and half outside, as if my partial presence might lessen his desire to see me.

"Anna, come in and take a seat." His tone was friendly, which confused me.

I sat down, my eyes scanning across his desk. It was the desk of a perfectionist. Papers were arranged like packs of cards still bound in their plastic wrappers. Every pen was separated by colour in a purpose-made pen holder. No tops were missing and each pen was carefully grouped with others of matching colour. He drummed his fingers on the table's surface before saying anything, and it made me think of a drumroll before the guillotine's blade was released.

"How are you getting on, Anna?"

"Fine, thank you," I said, knowing it was a prelude to something else.

"No problems then?"

"No," I said, slowly shaking my head, still wary of what was coming.

"I'm told you are friends with Rebecca?"

"Yes."

"I see." He paused, and I sensed he did not approve. "I wonder if you would be kind enough to give this to Rebecca?" He reached down to take a brown envelope from a drawer under the desk

"Yes, all right," I said, taking the envelope from him.

"Thank you." His *thank you* had an abruptness to it, leaving me in little doubt the meeting was over. His eyes left me and his attention went to a folder he began to open.

I left, as quietly as I had arrived.

Rebecca had deteriorated both in mind as well as body, and her wilted appearance shocked me. She had always been slim, but now there was a sickly gauntness to her features. Her cheekbones had become more pronounced, standing out sharply against a thin layer of skin. Her hair was unkempt and I doubted if she had washed it or herself for quite some time.

My attempts to discuss Pierre or the pregnancy were met

with a blank wall of silent indifference. I gave her the letter from Mr Wilkinson, but had to cajole her into opening it. It was as I feared. Rebecca had lost her job. Without making any comment, she folded the letter and put it back into the envelope. She placed it behind the clock on the mantelpiece, showing no concern for its contents or the implications that went with it.

I made her something to eat, persuaded her to wash, and then combed her long, beautiful hair. She let me fuss over her with the same indifferent attitude and appeared seemingly unconcerned whether I did anything or not. When I was finished, I stood back, telling her how beautiful she looked, but she did not respond, or smile, or indicate in any way at all that she felt the better for it.

"Anna." She paused as if wondering whether to continue. "Will you do something for me?"

"Of course, what is it you want?"

"Will you ask him something for me?"

"You mean Pierre?"

"Yes."

I nodded, wracked with guilt. I felt sure my eyes would betray me, but she was too preoccupied with her own despair to be in any way perceptive. "What do you want me to ask him?"

"I want to have an abortion. If he will give me the money, I'll never bother him again. Will you ask him that for me?"

I didn't answer for a few seconds, her words stopping my line of thought with an abrupt suddenness. "An abortion?" My words sounded so fragile that they could be snapped like a twig.

She looked down as if trying to summon the courage to look me in the eye. When her face did rise, it was a mixture of sadness and shame.

"Is that what you really want?"

"I've thought about it, Anna, don't think I haven't. How can I have a baby?" She looked around the room as if searching for words. "I can't even look after myself properly."

"But you wouldn't be alone. I'd help, and I'm sure others would, too."

"It's not just that. I couldn't live with the shame, I just couldn't."

"There's no shame. These things do happen." I reached

out to grasp her hand. Her fingers were icy cold.

She shook her head defiantly. "I can't go through that, the whispers, the sneers of disapproval. They'd label me. I know what they'd say...there goes the slut, the whore, a few drinks and she's anybody's."

"No one would say that."

"Yes they would, maybe not to my face, but that's what they would be thinking."

I did my best to make her look at it differently, but each suggestion was met with the same fear and dread of how she would be looked upon. I left, agreeing to meet Pierre on her behalf and to put forward her request.

Twenty-Five

I felt as if I was committing espionage as my eyes scanned the hotel register. I knew Pierre was due back the previous night and it did not take long to confirm it by finding his name in the book. He had checked in at eleven p.m., obviously after arriving on a late flight.

Going about my cleaning duties, my mind was torn with uncertainties and expectations that straddled the fine line between attainment and disappointment. Would our kiss be mentioned, or would we be like uncomfortable strangers, avoiding what we wanted to say and finding solace in pointless small talk? Rebecca's pitiful image came back to haunt me. For a moment, I despised her, cursed her for even existing, for complicating things by getting pregnant. No sooner had those thoughts emerged when I was consumed with guilt and remorse for my selfish considerations. I realised there could be nothing between me and Pierre. I told myself nothing good would come of it and it would only cause more heartbreak for Rebecca and probably for me, too. I made a decision to tell him what Rebecca asked me to say and no more. My promise would be honoured and my conscience would be clear.

The breakfast room was quiet, just a smattering of guests as one would expect for the time of year. There was no sign of him, and I assumed he slept late, tired from the previous day's travelling. The door to the kitchen swung open as one of the staff came out, and Rodrigo, catching my eye, grinned and gave a mock salute.

On the second floor, I made my way along the corridor, stopping only to clean rooms that had been occupied. I paused outside Pierre's door and put my ear against the wood panel. I could hear him moving around. I knocked, anxious to get it over with and be on my way. The door opened and he smiled. It was the smile of someone seeing an old friend, genuine and welcoming.

"Anna, come in."

He stood to one side and I walked in, hearing the door close behind me. I turned to spill out my rehearsed speech, but before I could utter a word, he reached out to grasp my shoulders and pull me toward him. He smelt of soap and his hair was wet with a strong scent of shampoo. All reasoning abandoned me when his lips touched mine. I felt myself go weak as his arms wrapped around me, pulling me closer. It was as if my mind and body had been possessed by a repressed urge that was finally unleashed. I felt him open my buttons one by one while my fingers worked clumsily to undo the knot on his dressing gown belt.

"Oh, Anna." His voice was little more than a whisper and the words seemed to tremble as if they were about to melt in the warm air of the room.

"Pierre...I don't think..." My voice trailed off as he lowered me back onto the bed. I felt myself enveloped by the duvet as it crept up around me like tepid bathwater. Then I felt his weight on me. He was kissing my neck and the sensation of hot breath behind my ear sent a tingle down the entire length of my body. I ran my hands down his back, feeling an irresistible urge to claw my nails across his bare skin. I shuddered as the palm of his hand caressed my inner thigh and gently worked its way up until I felt his fingers slowly moving across the front of my knickers as if to purposely heighten my anticipation.

"No, Pierre, get off me... We can't do this."

It wouldn't have taken much to dampen my resistance, probably one more kiss would have been enough to diminish my doubts and subdue my will. But he stood up, covering himself and trying awkwardly with one hand to pull back up his white robe.

"I'm sorry, Anna, I couldn't help myself. I haven't stopped thinking about you since the other night."

"When we kissed, you mean?" I sat up, feeling embarrassed as I tried to fix my uniform.

"Yes."

He looked down, seemingly ashamed to meet my eyes. His look of manly confidence had vanished, but it was another side to him that did not deter my view of him. If anything, I respected his display of humiliation.

"It's all right, Pierre. I thought of nothing else either."

His face rose until our eyes met. We stayed like that for a few moments, but in those brief seconds, silent dreams passed between us like an invisible river of emotions.

"What do we do now?" he asked with a relaxed smile.

His grin was infectious and my smile gave way to laughter. He sat beside me and wrapped his arm around my shoulder, pulling me close to him. I felt safe in his embrace, like nothing could ever hurt or make me sad again.

"Why did you come?" he asked.

"I wanted to talk to you about Rebecca." I hated saying her name at that instant, and the name itself seemed to crush the moment as if it was a hammer falling on a walnut. His arm fell back and the space between us widened a little like a crowbar had been used to pry us apart.

"I thought you came to see me."

"I did, I suppose... I mean, I wanted to come for my own reasons."

"Which are?"

"I'm not sure how to explain. I don't fully understand them myself."

"Then don't try," he said, shaking his head and reaching out to take my hand in his.

"I better get back to work," I said, getting to my feet.

"But you wanted to tell me something about Rebecca?"

"Yes, but not now. Can we meet later?"

He stood up, looking as if a renewed hope was driving him. "Will you come to dinner tomorrow night with me?"

"Dinner?"

"Yes. I discovered a wonderful little restaurant near Grafton Street. I only went there once, but felt self-conscious on my own. The waiter kept looking at me as if I was someone to be pitied. I've always hated eating alone. It would be nice to have company."

"I don't know," I said hesitantly, thinking I shouldn't, but knowing I wanted to.

He didn't say anything and waited while I made up my mind.

"All right," I said, sounding relieved I'd come to a decision.

He let out a long breath as if he had been holding it in until I answered.

Before I left, he held me tenderly and kissed me. We stayed entwined in each other's arms for several minutes, minutes that I wished would last forever.

Grandma had taken to her bed. She did not look well at all. Her face had a pale greyish colour to it and she would not eat. She looked thinner than ever lying in the bed with the covers pulled up tight to her chin. Grandpa and Peter were downstairs cleaning the kitchen. Grandma's state appeared to have caused them to call an uneasy truce.

"How are you feeling, Grandma?"

"I'll be all right. I just need some rest, that's all." Her voice was weak and every word seemed to require effort.

"Maybe we should call a doctor?"

"Oh no...no doctor." She looked terrified at the mere mention of it.

"Just to be on the safe side. Maybe he could prescribe something that will make you feel better."

"No, Anna. I don't want to see any doctors. Promise me you won't call one."

"But, Grandma—"

"No, promise me."

"All right, I promise."

I'd never seen her so scared and it worried me. I wasn't sure if she was afraid what a doctor might discover, or if she was just from a generation that didn't believe in physicians and modern medicine.

Grandpa, knowing I was in for the night, decided to go out to his Workers' Club. Peter said he would stay home, just in case she needed anything. I knew he had some money and his decision to stay impressed me. I made two mugs of hot chocolate and we sat in the parlour while Grandma slept upstairs.

"Do you think she will be all right?" I asked him.

"Yeah, she'll be fine. Don't worry about her."

"She looks awfully unwell. I can't help worrying. She won't hear of calling a doctor."

"Jasus, no!" He shook his head as if I'd made an obscene gesture. "She won't have anything to do with doctors, or hospitals."

"Why not?"

"No faith in them, I suppose. She says it's hard to find a doctor with experience. She thinks most of them are just out of college and haven't a clue what they are doing."

"But, that's silly."

"I know." He shrugged his shoulders. "But there's no telling her. She's convinced if she gets sent to hospital, she'll never get out again."

"But you must think she's bad if you are staying in."

He laughed. "Don't go jumping to conclusions. I just don't feel like going out tonight. It's as simple as that."

I watched him stir the last of his drink. I did not believe him.

"Peter?"

"What?"

"I promised to go out tomorrow night, but I don't want to go if Grandma is still unwell."

"A date?" He looked at me, squinting his eyes as if trying to see the answer.

"I wouldn't exactly call it a date."

"Either it's a date or it isn't, there's no in-between."

"All right, I suppose it is, but promise me you won't breathe a word to Grandpa."

"He can't tell you what to do, Anna. If you want to go on a date, that's your business."

"I know, but you know the way he'll go on. I'd just rather he didn't know."

"Well he won't hear it from me. I never tell the old bastard anything anyway."

"Will you stay in then, if I go out?"

"Tell you what, buy me a few bottles of ale and I'll stay in to watch the telly, all right?"

Twenty-Six

I packed my one and only dress into a bag and brought it to work. I could not face going back to Ignatius Road to get ready for my dinner date with Pierre. I would have loved to show it to Grandma, as it belonged to my mother, but I had no desire to endure Grandpa's inevitable rant about moralities and the virtues expected from a young unmarried girl.

While walking into the city centre, I worried about Grandma, but she seemed to have perked up during the day and devoured the toast I made before leaving. I also pondered on how to broach the topic with Pierre of Rebecca wanting an abortion. It would undoubtedly mar the evening, and I debated whether to mention it straight away or wait until the end of the night. By the time I reached the hotel, I was still undecided.

I carefully took out my dress in the staff room, intending to bring it to my locker, when Rodrigo walked in. His eyes widened and a row of pearly white teeth shined out at me.

"Señorita, what have we here?"

"I'm going out after work," I said.

"And some lucky muchacho will think himself a matador with such a pretty señorita on his arm."

I giggled before answering. "It's not really a proper date, Rodrigo."

"Oh my little chica, why do you lie to Rodrigo? When a muchacho asks a beautiful señorita to meet him, it is a date. At least in his eyes, believe me."

"You are making fun of me, I think."

"Oh no, no. I know what you think, Rodrigo joke all the time and never be serious. I know it not easy to picture, but Rodrigo was a handsome niño a long time ago, and all the pretty señoritas were proud to dance with Rodrigo."

"I believe you."

"Now you make fun of me, I think," he said, smiling more than ever. "Now tell me, my beautiful Anna, who is this lucky matador?"

"You wouldn't know him." I looked away for fear he would see the lie in my eyes.

"Ah, Frenchie!"

"How did..." I turned back to face him in surprise.

"You underestimate Rodrigo." He had a look of satisfaction, pleased he guessed correctly.

"But how could you know?"

"Simple observation, that is all. Every now and again, I sneak a peek out at the diners. It is something all chefs do. We like to see the faces of contentment as they enjoy our food. I saw Frenchie's eyes follow you across the room...and I saw the look you gave him before you disappeared from view. Rodrigo has seen these things many times before. You may think me a stupid peasant from the Basque country, but even a peasant can have experience of life."

"I never thought that of you."

"I know that, my sweet Anna. I'm just being dramatic. It's my way. But, tell me this..." His expression became guarded. "Isn't Frenchie Rebecca's hombre?"

"He was, but not anymore."

"I see, and now you want to sample the splendours of the wine country, taste the forbidden nectar of the gods, yes?"

"Do you think I'm wrong?"

"Right...wrong, they're two sides of the same coin. What's right for one person could be wrong for the next. It's not always so simple as right and wrong."

"I'm serious, Rodrigo."

"And so am I. There are times when nobody can tell you if you are truly wrong. That's something your own heart will answer for you. The heart always knows these things."

"But what if my heart doesn't know for sure?" I sat down, confused.

"Your heart always knows. It's a question of whether you

want to heed it."

"I just don't know if I'm making the right decision."

"Of course you're not."

"Why do you say that?"

"Because he's a Frenchie. Never trust the French, Anna. They're too full of themselves, too arrogant. They think the world adulates them because they make decent wine. They think Paris is the centre of the world."

"You're joking with me now."

"Who's joking? What you want is a nice Spanish boy. Now, you take my nephew, Pedro. He's..."

I spent ten minutes listening to Rodrigo promote his nephew before he remembered about something roasting in the oven and rushed out, returning to his world of clanging ladles and boiling pots.

I didn't have much time, but I used my lunch break to visit Rebecca. I woke her from a sleep and wondered if she'd been up all night or just lacked the enthusiasm to have gotten up this morning.

"Did you ask him?" she asked, with a strange look of indifference as to what the reply might be.

"No, not yet. I am meeting him after work."

She eyed me suspiciously.

"I told him you wanted to ask something of him, so we agreed to meet later." I spoke quickly, as if trying to justify myself.

"Why didn't you just ask him?"

"It was hardly something I could say in the breakfast room, was it?"

"No...I suppose not."

"How are you feeling?" I asked, hoping she wouldn't realise I was changing the subject.

"How do you think?" She shrugged. "I've no job, I'm pregnant, and I'm going to have to give up my flat."

"Why don't you go down to the welfare office? They will give you rent allowance until you find another job."

"I suppose...maybe tomorrow."

Her demeanour gave me the impression she wasn't going

to bother. I wanted to grab her by the shoulders and shake some sense into her. But I didn't. Time was against me and I had to hurry back to work.

There was a letter at reception with my name on it. The receptionist gave it to me and I scuttled away like a dog with a bone looking for somewhere private to read it. I expected it to be from Pierre, and I hoped he was not going to let me down. I was surprised when I realised it was not from him. It was from Robert Cleary. His handwriting was incredibly neat, and he even wrote his name and address on the top right corner of the page.

Robert Cleary
1 Hollybank Rd,
Dublin 9.

Dear Anna,
I thought it more prudent to send this letter to the hotel rather than Ignatius Road. There's much I would like to have said when we met, but as I'm sure you realise, I was quite shocked to find a daughter I never knew existed knocking on my door.
I've thought of little else since that day. I know it would be impossible to make up for all that has passed, and I am not going to try to make amends that would be both futile and false. What I do want so much is to get to know you as you are now. If you wish the same of me, it would make me very happy.
Yvonne and I are having a dinner party this coming Saturday. It will be an informal affair with just a few friends invited. We would love if you could attend. If you have a friend you would like to bring along, that would be fine.
There is no need to reply. If you decide to come, we are serving dinner at seven p.m. I do hope you can make it, but if not, we understand.
In the meantime, if there is anything at all that you need, please do not hesitate to contact me.

Yours sincerely,
Robert Cleary.

I reread the letter several times, convinced I had missed some hint of rejection, some indication that I was already forgotten and the note was merely a sign of good manners. I found nothing but a genuine invitation to build a relationship with my father. I slid the letter into the back of the locker and pondered on how complicated my life was becoming. I had to hide Robert from my grandparents, and Pierre from Rebecca and Grandpa. My head ached with the pressure of deceit and I sat down, wondering if it would be better to forsake everyone and just be alone.

When six o'clock came, I set about getting ready for my dinner date with Pierre. I tried on my dress and was shocked at how tight and short it was on me. I began to panic and would have abandoned all notions of going out if Petra had not come to my rescue. She walked slowly around me, her eyes scanning every inch of the black cotton fabric. She kept reaching out and tugging edges as she hummed and hawed to herself. Five minutes later, she was busy letting out the dress so it would fit better. I tried it on and looked at myself in the mirror. It hung better, but even still, I recoiled at seeing my image.

"It not right still," she said in a heavy Polish accent and shaking her head in disapproval. "You stay here. I get more something for you."

She left the room and I tried on my coat. Seeing my reflection, I lost all confidence and began to take off the dress.

"No, no, put back on, I fix good for you," Petra said as she walked back in.

I stood there, feeling like a Christmas tree as she circled me, adding and adjusting. She had gone to the storeroom behind the reception and borrowed clothes that had been left behind in rooms. They were usually kept for a month before they would be given to some charity. I don't think anyone ever returned to claim them.

I watched intently as she transformed me into something I wasn't. Stockings, black shoes, a navy cardigan and a beautiful dark coat later and I thought I was looking at someone else. I'd never worn makeup, but Petra expertly gave my face a light touch of colour. When she was finished, she stood back, proudly nodding at her creation like she was an artist having added the final touch to her masterpiece.

"I don't know what to say, Petra."

"It's nothing, nothing at all." She waved away my gratitude as if she was swatting flies.

Twenty-Seven

I sauntered as slowly as I could and took the long route to Grafton Street. I was determined not to be early and wanted to walk in as if my turning up was nothing more than a last minute decision made on a whim. But what if he wasn't there? I could feel the embarrassment of sitting alone, waiting for him to arrive, and having to endure the pitying glances of staff and diners alike.

I crossed the Ha'penny Bridge and saw the familiar face of the gypsy woman staring out from beneath her blanket hood. Her dark eyes were wide and hopeful in anticipation. I rummaged in my purse and found a fifty pence piece to drop into the small dish she held out. Her fingers were long and bony, almost skeletal-like. There was a clanging noise as the money rolled around the empty vessel.

"Bless you, child." She made the sign of the cross and kissed a crucifix that was hanging from her neck.

A feeling of goodness filled me as I continued on. I remembered back to Pierre giving money to a beggar huddled in a doorway. There was something about that charitable gesture that revealed a glimpse of his true character. But what about my true character? Could a person be charitable and selfish also? Was I being deceitful? Rodrigo's claim that *the heart always knows* came back to plague me. I thought about how I really felt as I walked through the narrow lanes of Temple Bar. I tried to look into my heart for answers. The more I thought about it, the more I felt I was doing nothing wrong. The only deed I was guilty of was being too cowardly to tell Rebecca. I eased my conscience by deciding to tell her as soon as the opportunity presented itself.

The restaurant was on the corner of Balfe Street, a small narrow road that was little more than a laneway swinging around in a curve from Grafton to Chatham Street. The Westbury Hotel towered over the restaurant from the other side and the hotel's doorman, dressed in a pristine uniform and a top hat, stood holding open the door of an expensive-looking black car. The car's gleaming metalwork reflected the orange streetlamps across its surface like shimmering stars in the night sky.

I peered in through the restaurant's window. Only half the tables were occupied and I saw Pierre sitting back, relaxed and at ease, chatting casually with the waiter who was adjusting a small floral arrangement centred on the table. I went in, but before the manager could offer me a table, Pierre stood up and practically rushed forward.

"Anna, I'm so happy you came."

I smiled in acknowledgement.

"You...you look wonderful."

"Thank you," I said, aware of my face reddening, but hoping it would not be noticeable in the low lighting.

He leaned forward and gave me a soft kiss on the cheek before taking my hand and leading me to the table. His hand felt warm around my cold fingers. He must have sensed this, as he rubbed my hands between his, first one and then the other.

"This is nice," I said, referring to the restaurant, unable to think of anything more creative to say.

"Yes, we French might produce the best wines, but you can't beat the Italians for food."

I laughed, thinking back to what Rodrigo had said about the French and their wine. He smiled, unsure of why his comment was so amusing.

My eyes widened at seeing the prices on the menu. I assumed he was paying as he did invite me. If his intention was to split the bill, then I could see myself washing dishes late into the night.

We both ordered the same meal, Spaghetti Bolognese, and Pierre asked for a bottle of Sangiovese wine, the brand rolling off his lips like well-rehearsed poetry. The waiter bowed gracefully and returned to display the label for approval.

"I was afraid you were not coming," he said.

"I'm sorry. I was a little late making my way here."

"You have made me very happy," he said, reaching out to hold my fingers in his.

"I wanted to come," I said, smiling.

"You said you needed to ask me something...about Rebecca?"

"Not now, it can wait until later."

He looked relieved. I suspected he felt as I did, that discussing her would be an uncomfortable distraction to the evening, and was hoping to get the subject over and done with, but was happy to postpone it as I suggested.

"How long will you be staying in Ireland?"

"Not long. A few weeks maybe."

"Then where will you be working?"

"I'm going back to France. My father wants me to take over the running of the vineyard."

"Really?"

"Yes, he's going to retire and I am the natural choice for taking over."

"Why is that?"

"You see, I have a brother, but he has no head for business and is happy living in Paris."

"And you do, have a head for business, I mean?"

"Well, yes, I'm no Rockefeller, but I love the vineyard like it was a woman, and I know wine. It is in my blood, you might say."

"I envy you," I said.

"In what way?"

"You are going to be doing something you love. Most people don't get that chance."

"And what would you love to do, Anna? If you had the choice."

"I don't know. I haven't discovered what I want yet."

"You can't be content working in the hotel."

"No, of course not. It's just a job to help me get started."

We finished the starter and the main course arrived. He looked at me, waiting for a reaction as I tried it. I think the pleasurable look on my face was enough as he leaned back in his chair, smiling with satisfaction.

"I told you the food was good. As I said, the Italians

make the best food."

"I'm inclined to agree, but don't let Rodrigo hear you saying that."

"Rodrigo?"

"He's the head chef at the Royal Dublin."

"I'll remember. Thanks for the tip." He raised his glass to mine. "Here's to finding what you want in life."

"Cheers." I clinked my glass against his.

"Anna, there's something I want to ask you."

"Yes?"

"How would you feel about visiting me in France?"

I didn't answer, unsure of what exactly he had in mind.

"I'm going to be honest with you." He leaned forward. It was either to keep our conversation private or to add weight to his suggestion. "It is not often one meets a woman of such rich substance, a woman that makes a man feel more alive than at any time in his life." He paused, maybe waiting for me to say something, but I was stuck for words. "Anna—"

"Yes?"

"I know in my heart that if you see our vineyard, you will fall in love with the country and never want to leave."

"Are you sure you mean the country?"

"I'd never be that presumptuous. A man cannot make a woman love him, but I am hoping that will come in time."

"I don't know want to say."

"Don't say anything. Just think about it. I am inviting you to visit Chateau de Flomlay as my guest. I'm not suggesting anything improper, just that you consider visiting...as a friend."

"All right, I will think about it."

We moved on to the desserts. My stomach felt as if it couldn't fit anymore in, but the menu, complete with images of ice creams whipped up and smothered in dripping cream, was too much to resist. I was thinking about his suggestion that I visit France. It sounded like a roundabout way of proposing to me. I was glad he put it the way he did. Had he produced a ring and fallen on one knee, I do believe I would have died of embarrassment.

Pierre paid the bill and we left the warm cosiness of the restaurant for the dark and cold streets outside.

"Would you like to walk for a while?" he asked.

"Yes, I think that would be a good idea after all I've

eaten."

Grafton Street was quiet and the tall buildings sheltered us from the brunt of the wind. We strolled arm-in-arm as I looked in the shop windows, marvelling at the fashion on display. A lone busker played a sombre melody on a harmonica, a small dog sitting by his side. We stopped to listen and it felt as if the mournful tune was recounting some great tragedy that had befallen the musician at some distant time in the past. When he finished, Pierre threw some coins into his cup.

"Merci."

"Etes-vous Française?"

"Oui oui, I am from Lyon."

"Est-ce que vous connaissez la chanson, Vent d'Est?"

"Oui, voulez-vous que je la joue pour vous?

"Oui, pour la dame."

"What did you say to him?" I asked.

"I asked him to play something special for you."

The busker took a few purposeful breaths and began to play a tune, the like of which I'd never heard before. Every note came slow and with meaning as if each individual sound was tearing a piece from his heart.

"What is it he's playing?"

"Vent D'est. It means wind from the east, or eastern wind. The song is about a Frenchman that is hopelessly in love with a beautiful Chinese girl. But she cannot return his love and, realising this, he writes a poem for her before departing."

"That sounds so sad."

"It is, but aren't the most touching songs always laden with heartbreak?"

"I wouldn't know."

I felt his arm tighten around my waist.

"Do you know the words to the poem, Pierre?"

"I think so...maybe."

"What are they?"

"Well, I can try, but I'll probably make a mess of the translation."

"Go on, try for me, please."

"All right, I'll try," he said, smiling at me.

The busker, hearing him recite the ode, slowed the tune and synchronised the sad air in keeping with Pierre's voice.

"An eastern wind swept over land, and against all tide,
And within its swirling mass, a lost flower cried.
In a far off land, earth to root – it did find,
And bestowed to the world, splendour, one of a kind.
Petals of silk and fragrance beyond decree,
An oriental flower reached forth to me.
Behold, I saw it blossom, and intoxicated by the scent,
Let beauty caress my soul, but found love only lent.
Alas, I let go, but to this day,
An eastern wind – upon my heart does weigh."

When the recital ended, a small group people clapped and Pierre, not realising he had an audience, became bashful and modest-looking. Each of the onlookers threw coins into the busker's dish and when Pierre tried to pay him, he waved him away, smiling as he indicated the half full bowl of coins. We bade the musician farewell and continued on our way.

"Why could the girl not return his love?" I asked, intrigued by the words of the poem.

"I don't know. The verse does not explain why. I think the author intended the listener to come to their own conclusions."

"And what do you think was the reason?"

"I've never really thought about it."

"You liar," I said, smiling so broadly my face must have looked as if it could crack in half.

"Why do you say that?"

"Because you knew the poem word for word, so you can't tell me you never thought about the reason."

"You have me there," he said, holding up his hands in mock surrender. "I believe her hand was promised to someone else. She did love him, maybe even more than he loved her, but she felt duty bound to marry the man her parents had promised her to."

"That's sad," I said. "I wonder if that was the reason."

"Can you think of something else, Anna?"

"I think…" I paused, putting together the story in my head. "I think she came from a poor village in China, whereas the Frenchman was from a prominent Parisian family. She knew if he took her as his wife, his social standing would suffer, and maybe lead to his downfall. While he was prepared to forsake everything for her, she loved him too much to let that happen. So, she hid her tears and rejected his love."

Pierre stopped walking and stared at me as if I was an apparition. "Anna, who would have known?"

"Known what?"

"That beneath the surface" —he caressed my cheek with the back of his fingers—"lies the heart and soul of an artist. I can see it now, an epic love story written by a genius."

"Now you are making fun of me."

"You could not be more mistaken."

I'd never seen him look so serious. He pulled me closer and his lips glided across mine, slow and seductively. He held me as if he was never going to let go and, during that brief moment, I don't think I ever wanted him to.

Twenty-Eight

I dreamt of green hills rolling gracefully into the distance. I could smell the sweet fragrance of a thousand grape vines, their scent carried on a warm summer breeze. I was running carelessly like a child through the endless rows of plants and feeling the heat of the sun on my face. The peaceful silence was broken only by the clicking of crickets and the song of a nightingale that graced the afternoon with his melody. Pierre was there, standing at the bottom of the hill, his shirt sleeves rolled up as he waved to me.

I ran down, struggling to keep control of my footing on the dry, sun-baked clay. When I reached him, he caught me in his arms and swung me around as if I was weightless. He brushed a strand of hair from my face and kissed me. I was safe in this place, and in his arms I was content. I woke happier than I had in quite a while.

Peter had honoured his promise and stayed home to watch over Grandma. She seemed to have recovered and, despite looking tired, she was up and cheery once again. Even Grandpa was not subjecting us to his usual morning rants, and whilst eating breakfast, I felt as if I had turned a corner in my life and found anything was possible.

It was a bright Saturday morning, and walking to Rebecca's flat, I rehearsed all I was going to say. Firstly, I was going to tell her about me and Pierre. Secondly, that she would have to ask him for money herself, as I didn't feel comfortable doing it. I realised it would probably spell the end of our friendship, and although it was not what I wanted, the fact was, I could no longer continue to live a lie. There were but-terflies in my stomach as I waited for an answer at the front door, but there was also a feeling of relief, relief that soon I would have no secrets from her. Several times I listened to the dull drone of the buzzer, but no answer came. I kept looking up, but no face appeared at the window. I was half-way down the steps and about to go home when the door creaked open. The young couple that had so often shuffled past me without a word were coming out.

"Are you lookin' for your friend?" the girl asked.

"Erm...yes," I answered awkwardly, surprised she had ac-tually spoken to me.

"She was taken away in an ambulance last night."

It took me a few seconds to answer, as my mind ab-sorbed her words. "Why, what happened?"

"I dunno." She shrugged and her boyfriend looked back at her, seemingly anxious to be on his way.

"Was she sick?"

"I said, I dunno." She looked irritated, as if I was a nui-sance.

"Do you know what hospital they took her to?"

She let out a long sigh and pursed her lips, giving me the impression this was the last question she was going to an-swer. "The Mater Hospital, I suppose. It's the closest."

I thanked her, but they already had their backs to me and were walking away. The girl lifted her arm in a half-hearted acknowledgement of my thank you.

I walked as fast as possible to the hospital. It was only one mile from Mountjoy Square, and I hoped it would be where she was, just as the girl suggested. All sorts of crazy thoughts were going through my mind. I knew she was de-pressed and I hoped she hadn't tried anything stupid.

The hospital was an old building on Eccles Street. Its fa-çade was finished with large granite blocks, and two wide stone stairwells curved up and around to meet at the double entrance doors, which would not have looked out of place in a cathedral. I gave Rebecca's name to the woman sitting be-hind a long, wooden reception desk. She pulled an index card from a plastic container and nodded to indicate she'd found the correct name.

"Visiting hours are from three to four p.m.," she said in a reprimanding voice.

"I didn't know. I only just found out she was brought here last night by ambulance. Please, she has no family, I'm sure she must be upset."

The woman frowned before answering. "Go on then. Second floor, St. Mary's ward."

I thanked her and made my way through the corridors, passing worried-looking relatives and doctors that seemed to jog rather than walk.

Rebecca was asleep. She had a bed in the middle of the ward, which, unlike the others, had no cards draped over the bedrail or flowers on the adjoining locker. She looked so sad even while sleeping. I reached out to hold her hand, and her fingers felt fragile between mine.

Sensing my touch, her eyes slowly opened. They stared at the ceiling for a while, as if her mind had not yet comprehended that she was awake. Then her head lolled toward me and her eyes widened at seeing me there.

"Anna." Her voice seemed heavy with weariness.

"I'm here. You're going to be all right now."

"How did you know I was here?"

"The girl living downstairs from you told me. What happened?"

She looked away, her eyes reddening.

"Rebecca?"

"I lost the baby." She looked back toward me, and I thought she might burst into tears at any moment.

"I'm so sorry. I don't know what to say."

She tried to smile. "You don't have to say anything. I'm just glad you're here."

"But what happened?"

"It's all a bit of a blur now. I woke up feeling weak and unwell. I thought I was in a fever and soaking in sweat, but when I turned on the lamp, I saw it was blood. I was so scared, I thought I was dying," she said, wiping a tear away with the back of her hand. "I managed to get dressed and go down to phone an ambulance. I remember crying over the phone and then I must have passed out, because the next thing I remember was waking up in the accident and emergency department."

"Thank God you called for help." I leaned over to hug her.

"I'm all right now. The doctor said I lost a lot of blood so they'd keep me in for twenty-four hours, just as a precaution."

"So, they'll send you home tonight?"

"No, tomorrow morning, I think. They only do their rounds in the mornings, so I'll have to wait until then."

"Is there anything I can get you?"

"No, it's not worth the bother. Did you speak to Pierre?"

"Erm, no, I never got the chance."

"Probably just as well. I suppose I should let him know what has happened. Do you think he might come and see me? Maybe he's not angry with me anymore."

"I don't know—"

"If I write him a letter, will you leave it at the hotel reception for me?"

I found myself agreeing, unable to tell her what had happened between me and the man she had set her sights on. Rebecca scribbled a note on some blank paper, folded it, and got an envelope from the woman in the next bed.

"Can you leave it for him this afternoon? That way, he'll have read it by tonight."

If only she knew. Pierre had agreed to accompany me to the dinner party my father and his girlfriend were hosting. I would be handing the note to him personally, probably watching his expression if he chose to read it there and then. I silently cursed myself for not saying something. But how could I? How could I explain to Rebecca as she lay recovering from a miscarriage that I had stolen her boyfriend? That would be the way she would see it, and thinking to myself, if the roles were reversed, that's how I would see it, too.

Twenty-Nine

The evening was cold and a lingering mist hung over the city like a wet veil. Pierre's grasp of my hand felt warm as our palms pressed together. We walked at little more than a snail's pace, not wanting to arrive before the appointed time for my father's dinner party. He was quiet and I did not pressure him for conversation. I had no idea he would take the news of Rebecca's miscarriage so hard. I was wrong not to foresee his grief. Regardless of what complications the future may have held, it would still have been his child, and a sense of loss for a life that would never exist had wounded his heart. I suddenly felt a pang of guilt for asking him to come with me.

"Pierre, if you would rather not go, it's all right, I understand."

"No," he said, shaking his head. "I want to go."

"No, you don't. You're just coming to please me."

"You are wrong, Anna. I do want to go. But not to please you, or for the reasons one normally attends such get-togethers."

"But, why then?"

"Because I know this is important to you and I want to be there to support you, to hold your hand, to be a foundation for your confidence."

"You are a good man, Pierre." I pursed my lips together as if I was about to shed a tear. It would have been a tear like one might shed at the end of a heart-warming movie.

"I am *your* man, Anna, if you will let me."

I wrapped my arms around his waist and buried my head

into his chest. He rocked me gently as though I was a child seeking comfort.

The house on Hollybank Road seemed to radiate an aura of cosiness. All the curtains were drawn, but through the downstairs drapes, a warm reddish glow flickered, promising comfort and warmth to those invited in. The surface of the varnished front door shone as it reflected the tawny glimmering of a street lamp. We walked up the steps and Pierre knocked.

The door opened inward and a middle-aged woman stood facing us, her long, dark hair shining below the hall light. She looked at me for a moment before speaking. "Anna?"

"Yes, are you Yvonne?"

"Yes, come in. Robert will be thrilled you came." She smiled, looking genuinely pleased to see me. She stood to one side. She was wearing an elegant cream evening gown with a hint of glitter in the fabric that sparkled every time she moved.

"This is my friend, Pierre."

"I'm very pleased to meet you, Pierre," she said while closing the door, looking relieved to shut out the cold night.

I was glad Pierre was with me and doubted I would have had the courage to attend on my own. I felt I could hide behind his poised manner and casual nature. He appeared unfazed meeting people and I envied his self-confidence.

Robert was standing at the fireplace, a wine glass in one hand and the other waving around as he was in an animated conversation with one of his guests. When he saw me, his eyes widened in delight, and with a sense of urgency he looked for somewhere to place the glass before coming to greet me.

"I can't tell you how much this means to me. Thank you so much for coming." He spoke with liveliness in his voice, obviously feeling less inhibited due to a few drinks. He wasn't drunk, or even tipsy, but there was no doubt his confidence had been bolstered by a drink or two.

I introduced Pierre, and Robert seemed pleasantly surprised he was French.

"Let me introduce you to everyone," Robert said.

He led me to the centre of the room, a proud smile on his face, as if he was showing off a treasured painting from a private collection. There were three couples, not including me and Pierre, or Robert and Yvonne. I shook hands with each of them, being introduced without any hesitation as his daughter. After the second introduction, I gave up trying to remember individual names, trusting I could get by without them. They were all teachers in one way or another, except for one woman who seemed fragile and noticeably quieter than the others. She was a librarian and was so timid she looked like a porcelain doll that might shatter into a hundred pieces should someone shout at her.

I watched Pierre move around the room, engaging in small talk and laughing when required. Although I was intimidated by the highbrow conversation and the academic tone to the evening, Pierre seemed to fit in to this small intellectual world with apparent effortlessness, swapping opinions and trading abstract ideas at will. When he talked, they did more than listen. They adopted a look of great seriousness, seeming to heed all he said as if he spoke with a profound experience that impressed them. Robert's friends were nice and not one raised an eyebrow when I told them I worked as a cleaner in a hotel. I had obviously been the topic of an earlier discussion because none of them had inquired about my background or asked which university I attended.

We left shortly after eleven. The dinner party was in full swing, but I wanted to talk to Pierre and that was impossible to do with any sense of privacy. Robert, now tipsy, his eyes wide and sparkling from half a bottle of wine, thanked me for coming. He thanked me profusely as if I had saved his life or accomplished some other fantastic deed on his behalf. We agreed to meet the following day for lunch as he said he desperately wanted to talk to me. He assured me there was nothing wrong and he simply wanted to spend some time with me. I agreed, not feeling at all uncomfortable about the arrangement.

Saying our goodbyes, we wandered out into the cold streets of Drumcondra. Wet leaves blanketed the ground and their brittle surfaces glistened under the ochre glow of streetlamps. Pierre lent me his arm after I nearly slipped on a cluster of damp leaves.

"I like your father."

"Do you?"

"Yes. There's an honesty about him that seems almost refreshing. I can tell you, Anna, in my work, I meet many people. One quickly gets to recognise the liars, the back stabbers, and the dreamers."

"The dreamers?"

"That's just my name for them. They are full of good intentions. In their eagerness to please, they will promise you everything. Unlike the liars, they truthfully mean to fulfill their promises, but they lack the gift of realisticness...is that a proper word?" he said, smiling.

I shrugged my shoulders. "Is there anyone good in your business?"

"Yes, of course, I just didn't mention them because we tend to think about the dishonest people more."

"You haven't said anything about Rebecca all night. Not since I gave you her letter." I held my breath after speaking, wondering if it was a mistake to bring up the subject.

"No." He paused, looking thoughtful before answering. "Her letter confused me, worried me, even."

"Worried you? In what way?"

"I'm sorry I left the letter back in my room." He patted his jacket pocket as he spoke.

"What did it say?"

"She wanted me to visit her. She said now the baby was gone, everything would be alright between us again."

"Anything else?"

"Not really. What worried me was how she mentioned the miscarriage so briefly, like one might mention some insignificant fact, like the weather."

"Are you going to visit her?"

"No. I told her before we were finished. Other than giving whatever support she needed for the baby, there was nothing else between us. Now there is no baby, there is no reason for me to see her. Please don't misunderstand me, Anna. I'm truly sorry for what has happened to her. It is something I would never have wished for. How it has happened, I think it's best I do not visit. I wrote her a letter explaining this and had it delivered to her address this afternoon."

I felt a wave of pity envelope me as I thought of Rebecca, sitting alone in her flat and reading his words of rejection.

"I'm assuming from what she wrote that she doesn't know about us," Pierre said.

"No, not yet. I meant to tell her, but I never found the right moment."

"Are you going to tell her?"

"Yes, of course. I'm not doing anything wrong, am I?"

"No, *we* are not." He stopped walking and turned to face me. "But we both know that's not how she will see it."

"I know. You are right, Pierre. But I'll have to tell her."

"I think it might cost you your friendship with her."

I nodded. "It probably will."

"I'm sorry, Anna. I did not plan for any of this."

"I know you didn't. Let's forget about it for tonight, okay?"

"Not another word." He put his arm around my shoulder and we began to walk again.

Ten minutes later, we were standing at the end of Ignatius Road. We kissed and waited, each as reluctant as the other to leave.

"I don't want to let you go," he said, his grip around my hand tightening.

"I know...I don't want to either, but there is nowhere to go."

"I want to hold you, Anna. To make love to you, to watch your eyes close as you fall asleep in my arms."

At that moment, listening to his voice and looking into his dark eyes, I wanted to be with him more than I'd ever wanted anything before. "I want that, Pierre, but I can't go back with you to the hotel."

In an instant, I felt myself being pulled toward the curb as Pierre waved his hand at a passing taxi. The driver swung to the side, much to the annoyance of another driver that beeped his horn before driving on.

"The Skylon Hotel," Pierre said as we slid across the back seat.

Five minutes later, we were standing outside the doors to the hotel.

"I can't go in there, Pierre," I said, looking shocked at the thought.

"Why not?"

"I'd be too embarrassed, that's why."

"Embarrassed...why?"

"Because, they'll know why we want a room. And I'll feel like a prostitute, standing in the reception while you book one."

He laughed. "Oh, Anna. Trust me, I know just what to

say."

I was still hesitant and he pulled me inside and toward the desk. I stood back, feeling dreadful embarrassment while he talked.

I listened as he told the receptionist how we had just arrived from the airport, but our luggage was delayed. She looked on us with pity as he spoke. I heard him mention something about his wife not knowing any English, which actually gave me some confidence as I found I could look the receptionist in the eye without feeling the pressure to talk. He paid for the room and requested if our luggage arrived, would they sent it straight up to us, regardless of the time. It all happened so quickly, and before I knew it, we were alone in our room and smiling at one another.

We didn't speak. He took me in his arms as if I weighed nothing and lowered me back onto the bed. I sank into the soft mattress as he lay down beside me. The sensation of his warm breath on my neck filled me with an ecstasy that was new to me.

I didn't remember our clothes coming off. His naked skin pressed against mine aroused me beyond anything I had experienced before. My breasts seemed to lose themselves in his hands. Suddenly, he sat up and swung his legs out of the bed.

"What's wrong?" I asked.

"Nothing," he said, looking embarrassed.

And then I realised he was struggling to rip open a condom packet. I giggled and he smiled back and me, relieved I had lightened the awkwardness of the moment.

"Pierre..." My voice trailed off as I found it hard to continue.

"Yes, Anna? Is something wrong?"

"No, it's just that..." Again, my words failed me.

He reached out and gently stroked my arm. "We don't have to do this if you don't want to."

"No, I do want to. It's just that, I've never done this before."

"Haven't you?" He looked genuinely surprised.

I shook my head.

"There's nothing to worry about." He spoke as he slid in under the duvet.

"I know." A strange sense of relaxation swept over me

and I lay back, feeling happy I was giving him complete freedom of my body.

He rolled over onto me, letting most of his weight rest on his elbows on either side of me. My eyes closed and I quivered as his fingertips ran across my chest with a light touch that was electrifying. I felt his breath behind my ear and then his lips caressed mine before our tongues met. I let out a soft moan when I felt him push into me. It was a slow and gentle motion as each time he seemed to push in farther and farther. He whispered my name several times with a tremble that appeared to be caused by immense pleasure. My arms tightened around his back and his thrusts became faster. I felt pain, but it was a discomfort I didn't want to stop. My fingernails dug into his back as he continued to push into me. I was as the point of feeling I was about to explode when his body shook and he let out a loud groan of contentment. Then, his whole form relaxed and he rolled off me. Our eyes met in the half-light and held each other's gazes for what seemed an eternity until we both drifted off into a contented sleep.

Thirty

Grandma was unusually quiet. Her face was pale and her eyes had a sort of glazed-over look. She insisted she was fine and seemed irritated at me for asking.

Despite the apparent concern he had shown earlier, Grandpa appeared to tire of her being ill and became blatantly unconcerned about her. He left to go to eleven o'clock mass, as was his routine every Sunday. It was also his habit to go for a drink after the service, and it would be mid-afternoon before he returned. It was always the same and he rarely deviated from his holy day ritual. He would return in the late afternoon smelling of whiskey. His cold eyes would ungratefully scan the kitchen for his dinner, which without fail, would always be there.

I left at eleven-thirty, intending to call on Rebecca before meeting Robert for lunch in the Kylemore cafe on the corner of Abbey Street and O'Connell Street. I assumed she would be home from the hospital. If she wasn't, I'd call in to visit her on my way home in the afternoon. I was dreading the conversation we would have. If she was home, she would have read Pierre's letter, explaining how he no longer wanted anything to do with her. And on top of that, I had to tell her about Pierre and me.

There was no answer when I called. I could have been mistaken, but I was convinced I saw the dark outline of a person behind the faded net curtain. The figure was motion-less, silently staring out as I looked back from across the road. I only lingered a few minutes before leaving, still unsure if the obscure figure was a figment of my imagination.

I walked around the Garden of Remembrance to put in the time until one o'clock. It was a sombre park, dotted with stone plaques and statues dedicated to thousands of ghosts destined to live forever in name if nothing else. An old and sad-looking man sat on one of the benches. He kept reaching into a plastic bag and flinging handfuls of breadcrumbs into the air. They fell like snow and then settled on the ground like confetti outside a church door. The scraps of bread did not remain long. Pigeons congregated as if appearing out of thin air to feast on the old man's generosity. I watched him for a while, imagining his life and his unchanging routine before returning to a cold and lonely bedsit. For that was where my imagination pictured him living. I suspected if I returned any day of the week around this time, I would find him there, alone with only the birds for company.

Robert was early, looking a little nervous while waiting for me. When I arrived, he smiled and hugged me. His hug spoke volumes. It was a warm embrace that showed relief, relief that I'd come and had not changed my mind. It lasted longer than a hug normally did. Although, how a hug's duration in such circumstances was determined, I had no idea. It was perhaps to compensate for those missing eighteen years, years that were lost to him forever. We sat down and ordered lunch. He stared at me, his face displaying deep emotion.

"Thank you for coming last night," he said, his face expressing the gratitude as much as his words.

"I enjoyed it, and so did Pierre."

"He's a nice chap, that Pierre. Have you known him long?"

"A month or two, that's all."

"He's older than you." Robert's statement seemed more like a question as he waited for me to reply. I didn't answer. I looked at him, as I wondered what way he meant it.

"Oh gosh, I'm sorry, Anna. I didn't mean it like that. It was just an observation, that's all," he said, looking embarrassed.

"That's all right." I spoke without answering his question. "I like Yvonne. Have you two been together long?"

"About five years."

"Wow, that's great."

"Anna," he said, starting to take on a serious expression. "One of the reasons I wanted to talk to you was because of your future."

"My future?"

"Yes, and please don't take offence, I know I have no entitlements whatsoever when it comes to you or your life, but if you could just hear me out."

"All right, I'm listening."

"Do you remember Harold Bunting? He was at the dinner party the other night."

"The man with the bushy moustache?" I could have said the bald guy with the potbelly, but thought it better to be diplomatic.

"Yes, that was him. Anyway, Harold is on the board of Winchester College in London. Have you heard of it?"

I shook my head.

"Well, he seemed impressed by you the other night and, well to be honest, he was a bit taken aback when he heard you weren't attending any university."

"I don't understand what you are saying?"

He leaned in closer, pushing his coffee cup aside and looking excited. "Well, let me cut to the chase. Harold has told me there's a place for you in Winchester College if you want it."

"I still don't understand."

"You could do a degree, get a good qualification behind you."

"But I can't afford anything like that."

"No, but I can," he said.

"Look, Robert, I'm very grateful, but I can't accept anything like that from you."

"I'm not taking no for an answer." He waved his hands in a dismissive manner.

"You don't owe me anything, Robert. I've told you that before."

"So you've said, but this is something I want to do, not something I feel obliged to do."

"And what does Yvonne think of you doing this?"

He looked a little embarrassed for a moment. "Well, to be perfectly honest, it was her idea."

"Her idea?"

"Yes, she suggested it to Harold, who had no objections, and then she told me. But, in my defence, I do believe I would have thought of it sooner or later."

"I don't know—"

"Just think it over, that's all I ask. There's no hurry in making a decision."

"All right, I will. Thank you."

We ordered more tea and talked for over an hour. The more time I spent with him, the more I liked him. It still didn't feel like he was my father, but more like a friend I hadn't seen for years.

On the way home, I called into the hospital. It was not a surprise when the nurse told me Rebecca had been discharged that morning. I *had* seen her behind the curtain and despite letting myself think I had been fooled by the shadows, deep down, I knew what I had seen. As I walked back down the enormous steps of the hospital entrance, I made a decision. Obviously, she had read Pierre's letter. I decided not to call on her. My visit would only heap more bad news upon her. As I made my way to the main road, I wondered if I was simply taking the coward's way out. Whether I was or not, one thing was for certain, I felt as if a huge weight had been lifted from my shoulders.

Peter opened the door before I could push the key in. His face was filled with panic, and I held my breath, wondering what was wrong.

"It's Mother," he blurted out. "She's not well, Anna. I don't know what to do."

She was sitting by the fire in the parlour. Her eyes were heavy and despite the red glow from the fire, her face had a green tint to it. For a moment, I thought she was dead, but then her eyes moved slowly toward me. She seemed unable to speak.

"Peter, call an ambulance, now!"

"But she told me she doesn't want to go anywhere near a hospital."

"For God's sake, Peter, call a bloody ambulance. Just do as I tell you."

He was startled by my tone and without any further argument, he hurried out to the hall.

"It's all right, Grandma. We're going to get you sorted

out. Don't you worry about a thing." I spoke softly, trying to reassure her, but she didn't seem to be able to hear me. Nevertheless, I continued to whisper soft words of reassurance into her ear as Peter nervously walked to and fro, waiting for the ambulance.

Thirty-One

A cold breeze met us when we came out of the hospital. Neither of us spoke, both of us numbed by night's events. I stood quietly while Peter hailed a taxi from across the street. The driver seemed to register our profound sense of loss as we got into the backseat. He did not speak during the short trip, which was out of character for any Dublin taxi driver.

I stared blankly out the window at the passing people and buildings. The scene outside was a dreary blur as rain-water rolled down the glass, distorting everyone and every-thing. I tried to recall the doctor's words, but they swam around my head, like ill-fitting pieces of a jigsaw.

Grandpa was home. Peter had phoned him before we left, and he stood waiting in the kitchen, his stern face moderated by grief. He began to cry, asking how he would manage with-out her. We consoled him with words, but may God forgive me, because I silently cursed him and his crocodile tears.

We sat at the kitchen table and I did my best to repeat everything the doctor had said. I struggled to remember what they had told me and tried to reorganise their words into sentences we could understand. Grandpa sat nodding like one of those stupid office desk toys. Peter just stared at me, looking attentive, but I suspect, unable to comprehend much of what I was saying.

"The doctor said she had an aneurism on her aorta. Ac-cording to him, it was probably leaking for a while and that's why she was so unwell lately."

"I told her to go to a doctor." Grandpa scowled and

leaned back with a smug look of *I told you so* across his face.

"I asked them about that. If she had have gone sooner, I mean."

"And what did they say?" Grandpa smiled, as if waiting for conformation of his *told you so* comment.

"They said it would have made no difference, because of the size of the aneurism and her age. He said operating would not have been an option."

"I see...I see," Grandpa said, leaning forward to absorb the information.

Peter did not speak. He was still shocked, and Grandma's death had not sunk in on him yet. He left the house shortly after, seeking to drown his sorrows and drink the pain away.

I went back to the hospital with Grandpa to see her body. A nurse brought us through a labyrinth of quiet, narrow corridors, and I felt as if we were going to a secret place that no one with a choice would choose to visit. We arrived at the mortuary, which seemed to be at the back of the building. It was ironic, I thought. People came in the front door, and if they were unlucky, they left by the back. The nurse introduced us to a woman called Doris, who told us she was a hospital liaison worker, and it was her job to help families with questions and anything else they might need at a time like this. She was a pleasant woman, her voice mimicking the solemnness of the occasion.

Grandpa seemed to respect anyone who had an inkling of authority and kept nodding in agreement with anything she said. She led us into the room where Grandma's body was and then left us in privacy.

The coffin was open and in the middle of the room. When he saw her, he crumbled a little, suddenly looking older and less threatening as his harsh façade ebbed.

I stood quietly, looking at her face, which seemed so thin and frail. I reached out to touch her hand and held her fingers between mine for a few moments. Tears filled my eyes and I wept quietly as I wished we could have had more time before she had to go. Grandpa did not say anything and I forgot about his presence as I leaned down to kiss her on the forehead.

"Goodbye, Grandma...and thank you," I whispered into her ear before leaving the room to wait outside.

Doris was there waiting. She asked me questions and offered words of comfort, but I was too stunned to take in what she was saying.

Grandpa came out and I sat down, leaving him to talk with Doris. "I've lost my wife," I heard him say as he rubbed his eyes with a handkerchief.

"You poor man," Doris said, putting an arm lightly around his shoulders.

He had his back to me and I could see his shoulders jerking up and down accompanied by low sobs. I lacked pity for him. It was something I would keep to myself, but behind the sad front was a mean man with no realisation of how badly he had treated her when she was alive.

Peter vanished for two days and two nights, only returning on the morning of the funeral. I was angry about his absence, but held my tongue because of the day. He had played no part in the funeral arrangements, simply returning and assuming all the work was done. It exemplified his selfish manner just perfectly.

Grandpa was basking in the role of the grieving widower, being consoled and pitied by friends and neighbours. "She was a lovely woman," was one of the phrases I heard repeated over and over again. Grandpa also used the same phrase a few times, but I didn't think he would ever know just how wonderful she really was.

Life slowly found its own routine in the weeks after the funeral. While Grandpa's foul moods did not dissipate, he surprised me by cooking his own meals, and Peter's, too. He did not include me in his cooking. I was expected to look after myself, which was actually a relief as it meant less interaction with him. I ate at the hotel. Every day, Rodrigo made sure I had a hearty meal before I left. He continued his jovial criticisms of Pierre and all things French. Likewise, he never missed an opportunity to promote his nephew as a suitable marriage candidate.

Any feeling that seventy-six Ignatius Road was a home to me quickly ebbed away. I was nothing more than a lodger that came and went outside of working hours. Peter drank more and more. He was regularly missing for two and three days at a time. Where he went, I had no idea, for he rarely had much money. Whenever I saw him, his appearance had gotten worse. His clothes were dirty and becoming more threadbare all the time. He was losing weight, his prominent cheekbones being the most noticeable feature of his weight loss.

The three of us lived like strangers in the house. When Grandma passed away, any soul the house possessed died with her. All that was left was a building in which we came and went whenever we weren't sleeping. I tried to avoid the house as much as was feasibly possible. When I wasn't working, I spent most of my time in the company of Pierre. Each night he brought me somewhere different. When we tired of the picture houses and restaurants, we explored the city. It never ceased to amaze me when we found something new, a small gallery or an antique shop filled with curiosities hidden down narrow streets that often seemed like a maze.

We visited all the great churches and cathedrals in the city. In Christ Church, we roamed the medieval tunnels that were a warren of passageways and tombs. When we came back up, a service was taking place and the magnificent organ bellowed out sweet music that echoed through the entire structure. A priest, dressed in white and purple garb, led the choir, and their voices were those of angels singing from Heaven.

In the weeks following Grandma's death, I was floundering between happiness and sorrowfulness. My times with Pierre were the only times I felt truly happy during those passing weeks. While he did not pursue the topic, I was beginning to think that a life with him in the Bordeaux country was going to be my future. Each day my feelings for him grew stronger, and each day, I seemed to know and understand him a little more.

Thirty-Two

Three weeks had passed since Pierre sent his letter to Rebecca. During that period, I called at her door three times, each time getting no reply. I knew she had been home. Looking up at her window, I could see shadows fuelled by the fire flickering back and forth against the curtains. There was little doubt in my mind that she knew about me and Pierre, and I resigned myself to the fact that our friendship was over. It was for that reason I was surprised when Rodrigo told me she had called to the hotel looking for me. It had been the previous day, and it happened to be my day off.

"Did she say anything?" I asked Rodrigo.

"She didn't say anything other than ask for you. When I told her you were on a day off, she turned and left in a great hurry as if the devil himself was after her."

I didn't say anything at first. Rodrigo pursed his lips, looking worried and like he wanted to add something else but was wary of saying it.

"What's wrong, Rodrigo?"

"Oh, Anna, my sweet chica, my heart ached at seeing her."

"What do you mean?"

"She looked so troubled it frightened me. I asked if she wanted something to eat, but she did not even answer me, just hurried away." He pinched the base of his nose and closed his eyes tight to show his despair.

For the rest of the day, I was unable to rid myself of the troubled image Rodrigo had described. When six o'clock finally came, I left the hotel and made my way to Gardiner Street. As with my previous visits, there was no reply. But this time, I sensed she was not home. It wasn't just the darkness through the window. There seemed something desolate beyond the glass, something that gave me a feeling I could not easily put into words.

I gave up and went home. The moment I pushed open the front door, I sensed the tense atmosphere even before hearing the raised voices of Grandpa and Peter in the kitchen. I should have gone straight up to my room where I could hide, but I didn't. Unsure of what was wrong, I went into the kitchen.

Peter's face was bright red and there was madness in his eyes, like he might explode at any moment. Grandpa looked equally angry, but appeared more in control of himself, like feeling fury was second nature to him. They both glanced at me for the briefest of moments and then turned back to face each another.

"I *haven't got* any money," Peter said, saying it as if he was repeating himself.

"And we know the reason for that, don't we?" Grandpa said, his voice mimicking a sarcastic tone.

Peter did not answer.

"Because you pissed your money up against a wall, that's why!"

Peter looked even more furious, but he still did not reply to Grandpa's ranting.

"Everyone has to pay their way in this house." Grandpa turned his head toward me as he spoke. "Even *she* hands up money every week."

I shuddered as he used the word *she* rather than my name. He stressed the word with such venom, such distain, that my blood ran ice-cold. In that moment when he spoke, I felt as if I was something unclean and to be treated with no respect.

I left the room. They continued to shout at each another, paying no heed to my leaving. In my bedroom, I pulled the blankets over my head. It did not block out their raised voices, merely muffling the noise and making it sound like a far off television set. It wasn't long before I heard Peter storming out of the house, slamming the door behind him with such force that the whole house vibrated. After that, there was silence, and eventually, sleep came to me.

I waited for Pierre under the clock of Cleary's department store. It was almost seven in the evening and I had arrived before him. There were others there, waiting to meet boyfriends and girlfriends alike. It was a popular location for lovers to meet.

I looked around, studying the scattering of people waiting. Most were glancing up and down the street, looking out for the impending arrival of their partners. Some had a look of apprehension, making me think they were the ones that were on a first date. Others looked confident and without any worries. These were obviously the ones that had been in longer relationships and had probably met in this prearranged place many times before. I felt I belonged with the latter group. I was waiting for someone I felt comfortable with, someone I had come to know quite well.

"A penny for your thoughts?" Pierre's voice took me by surprise. He was smiling when I turned to face him. I didn't say anything as I stepped forward and pressed my face against his firm chest. His arms wrapped around me and as his embrace tightened. I felt safe, and I felt wanted.

We walked without deciding on where we should go. At O'Connell Street Bridge, we turned and walked up along the quays. There were numerous cargo boats tied along the wharf and merchant seamen were coming and going from their respective ships. They were not hard to identify. They were lonely-looking men with faces hardened from the sea breeze.

We went into a small cafe facing the water's edge. A smell of grilled food wafted out the door as we entered. We asked for coffee and sat at the window so we could watch boats making their way down the river and out into the bay.

"I leave Dublin in two weeks," Pierre said, his fingers lightly wrapping themselves around mine. There was a moment of silence as he waited for me to say something, but I wasn't sure how to answer. "Anna?"

"Yes?"

"You know what I'm going to ask, don't you?"

"Yes, I think so."

"Come with me, Anna."

"To France?"

"Yes, come with me." His fingers tightened their clasp of my hand.

"I...don't know."

"Why not? You must know by now that my heart belongs to you."

"I know. It's just that Robert has offered to help me get into college in London, and I'm thinking about it."

"I see," he said. His voice did not echo disappointment, but rather deep thought as he contemplated what I had said.

"I don't know what to do, Pierre, I really don't. I'm so confused right now. What do you think I should do?"

"How can I answer that? I know what *I want* you to do, but as for what you *should do*? Only you can decide that."

"Can we talk about this later?" I asked, feeling the seriousness of the topic press down on me with the weight of a heavy boulder.

"Of course." He leaned over to kiss me on the cheek.

"Rebecca called to the hotel a few days ago and was asking for me." Rebecca was not a topic I wanted to bring up, but I was anxious to change the subject, and she was the first thing I thought of.

"What did she want?"

"I don't know. I wasn't there, but Rodrigo said she seemed troubled. He tried talking to her, but she practically ran off."

"Do you think Rodrigo could be mistaken?"

"About what?"

"About her being troubled?"

"I don't think so. He seemed quite worried about her."

"She didn't come back?"

"No. I called to her flat, but there was no sign of her."

He dug through his coat pockets with a sense of urgency.

"What are you looking for?"

"I didn't mention it before," he said, still rummaging through his coat. "Rebecca slipped a note under my door the other day."

"What did it say?"

"Wait, I have it here somewhere." A moment later, he pulled out a crumpled piece of paper and put it on the table, ironing out the creases with his fist. "I thought nothing of it at the time." He turned it around for me to read. It was a short note, the writing resembling more of a scrawl.

Dear Pierre,

I am sorry if I have caused you any trouble. I know I was wrong and I want you to know I won't ever bother you again.

Her name was signed at the bottom.

"I'm sorry for not mentioning it. It seemed so insignificant that I forgot about it."

"Until now?"

"Well, yes. After hearing what Rodrigo said, I am seeing this note in a whole new light."

"What are you talking about, Pierre?"

He didn't answer, but his look grew more grave, and slowly it came to me just what he was thinking.

"You don't think..." My words trailed off as I was unable to say it.

"I don't know. Look, Anna, I'm sure we are jumping to the wrong conclusion here, but—"

"But what?" I interrupted him, becoming more alarmed every second. "You don't think she would do anything stupid, do you?"

He didn't answer, but the look he gave me displayed exactly what he was thinking.

We grabbed our coats and left. Outside the sky had darkened and there was a distant rumbling far out to sea as storm clouds gathered. I could not help but feel it was an ominous sign.

Thirty-Three

Once again, there was no reply from the bell. I pressed the button so hard my finger began to hurt. Pierre stepped forward and banged on the door with his fist. He kept pounding and small flakes of white paint broke off its surface. After a few minutes, the door was opened by one of the tenants, an Indian man with a turban wrapped tight around his head. Pierre walked straight past him, almost pushing him out of the way. I followed behind, mumbling an apology to the man who looked at me in a bewildered fashion.

Pierre ran straight up the stairs, taking three and four steps at a time. I had only reached the first landing when I heard him knocking and calling out her name. When I reached the top floor, he turned to me and said, "She's not answering."

"You don't really think she would have harmed herself?" I said.

"I don't know what to think."

I heard someone behind us and turned to see the young couple from the floor below. They stood on the top step, staring at us as if we were two crazy people.

"Have you seen Rebecca lately?" I asked them.

They didn't answer.

"Rebecca...you know, my friend? She lives here."

My words seemed to take a while to sink into their minds. Their eyes were wide and staring, and I got the distinct impression they were high from taking drugs. They exchanged glances before the girl answered.

"We haven't seen her for a few days."

"Right, that's it," Pierre said. Before I realised what he had in mind, he took a step back and kicked the door in. It gave way easily. The room was in darkness. I walked in behind him and tried the light switch, but nothing happened.

"No money in the meter?" the girl suggested.

I rummaged in my pocket and found a fifty pence piece. There was a clunk as the money fell into the slot and the room lit up.

She wasn't there. The room was a mess, the bed unmade, the fireplace full of cold ashes. Clothes were strewn about the room as if someone was frantically trying to find something.

"Thank God," I said with a sigh of relief.

"But where is she?" Pierre said, holding his hands up whilst continuing to look around the room. "It looks like she hasn't been here for a few days."

I turned to the couple, who had advanced to the door and were sticking their heads in, still wondering what all the fuss was about. "And you definitely haven't seen her in the last few days?" I asked them.

"Definitely not," the guy said. "Even if we didn't see her, our flat is right below. We can hear her walking about."

"That's right," the girl said. "The floorboards in this house creak somethin' awful, they do."

Pierre repaired the broken lock, using a kitchen knife as a screwdriver. I scribbled a note and stuck it to the outside of her door before we left. We left with an overwhelming feeling of hopelessness. There was nothing else to be done except wait and hope she contacted one of us.

Pierre walked me home. The thunderstorm had crept in over the city while we were in Rebecca's flat. The streets became enveloped in an ominous darkness as black clouds tumbled across the night sky.

There was a sudden flash followed by a sharp rumble that felt as if it would go on forever. The very air itself seemed to be crackling all around, and I could feel the strange sensation of static surround us like an invisible electric fence. Drops of rain began to hit the ground with a gentle pattering sound, but it quickly turned into a deluge. The rain was striking the ground with such force that the drops bounced back into the air after impact.

We hurried into the nearest pub for shelter. Our coats were already saturated and we hung them over the backs of chairs to dry out.

"I'll get us some drinks while we let the storm pass," Pierre said.

I waited, watching the street through the window. It was like a macabre firework display as the grey buildings became illuminated with each flash of lightning.

Pierre returned and we talked about the situation concerning Rebecca.

"Maybe I should go to the Garda station?" I suggested.

"And tell them what?"

"About our fears for Rebecca."

"I don't know...let's look at the evidence. She sent me a note to apologize and say she won't bother me again. I can't see them taking us seriously, can you?"

"No, I suppose not, when you put it like that. But I feel so helpless doing nothing. You think there's more to that letter than just an apology, don't you?"

He didn't answer straight away. He bit his bottom lip and adopted a look of great apprehension. I don't think he wanted to voice his fears.

"Your look says it all, Pierre. We have to go to the station. Even if they don't think there is anything to it, we still have to try."

"All right," he agreed, putting down his drink and peering out the window. "The rain is easing off. Do you know where the nearest Garda station is?"

"Thank you." I reached out to hold his hand and felt my fingers warming as his closed around mine.

We walked along wet pavements, listening to the water running along the gutters and down the roadside drains. Ten minutes later, we were standing in the public office of the local Garda station. The lobby was cold in appearance, the walls a bleak, dirty cream colour, and the whitewashed ceiling had paint peeling off in great chunks. There was no one behind the counter and a moth flew around the bare lightbulb above us, its shadow dancing across the walls like a giant bat.

I pressed the buzzer, and after a few minutes, a sergeant came out, his uniform clean but crumpled as if he had been dozing in a chair.

He listened patiently and attentively as I explained the

situation and our fears for Rebecca's well-being. He nodded occasionally and didn't interrupt, but waited for me to finish.

"So," he said with a heavy rural accent. "Your friend, she never actually said anything about harming herself?"

Pierre looked at me and I realised he was struggling to understand the sergeant's brogue.

"No," I said. "But we haven't seen her for a couple of weeks."

"And you, sir." He looked at Pierre. "Do you think it's possible this girl might do something to harm herself?"

Pierre stared at him for a moment as he tried to understand the question. Then he looked at me as if apologising for what he was about to say.

"Yes, sergeant, I'm afraid I do think just that."

"Hmm... What's her address again?" he asked while picking up a pen and paper.

We repeated the details for him as he wrote them down.

"Now, let me get this straight," he said, looking from Pierre to me and back to Pierre again. "She is your friend, miss...and she *was* your girlfriend, Mr Beaufort, is that right?"

"Yes," Pierre said while I nodded.

"And now..." His attention turned to me. "Now, Mr Beaufort is your boyfriend, is that right?"

I nodded again, feeling too ashamed to speak.

"I see," he said.

There was a moment's silence that seemed to last a lifetime as his eyes scanned his notes. Pierre's grip tightened around my hand as we waited to see if he was willing to take the matter seriously or not.

"Now, miss, I want you to go home and not to worry. As you said, it's been some weeks since you have seen your friend. I'm sure she'll turn up tomorrow or the next day safe and sound."

"So you're not going to do anything?" Pierre asked, the frustration evident in his voice.

"On the contrary, I'll send a car around to her house and have one of our men talk to the other tenants. Maybe one of them might know where she has gone. But other than that, there's not much we can for the moment."

"That would be great, thank you so much," I said, delighted that something would be done.

"In the meantime, miss, please go home and try not to

fret. If your friend contacts you, drop in and let me know, all right?"

Once again, we set off in the direction of Ignatius Road. We took a detour to walk past Rebecca's house. As we passed by on the opposite side of the road, we looked up at the curtains that were still in the same half-drawn position as before. There was no light on and the darkened window sent a foreboding chill down my spine.

Thirty-Four

Each day that passed after our visit to the Garda station had a strange phoniness about it. Until word came from Rebecca, the agony of waiting seemed to smother all other events. I felt like I was living in a bubble, surrounded by a cloud of uncertainty that would not evaporate until news came. Not a day passed that I didn't call to her flat, but nothing changed. The curtains remained in the same half-drawn position. On a few of the visits, I managed to talk to some of the residents as they were coming or going from the house. Their replies were always the same—no one had seen Rebecca recently.

I shared my worries to Robert Cleary. We met regularly, usually twice a week for coffee or lunch. He was a good listener. It seemed to come naturally to him, which surprised me as I'd always found that teachers normally liked to talk more than they listened.

Another thing I liked about him was that he would tell me the truth as he saw it. He agreed with my worst fears about Rebecca's well-being. He didn't use elegantly contrived arguments to convince me I shouldn't worry as Pierre had done. He put it quite bluntly that Rebecca's letter and subsequent disappearance was a matter for grave concern. I appreciated that rather than have someone fill me with false hopes.

"Have you thought any more about going to college in London?" he asked.

"I'm still thinking about it."

"There's something else I wanted to talk to you about, but I'm not sure how you will feel about it."

I could see he was hesitant about continuing, so I lightened the moment for him by laughing and saying, "Well I don't know either unless you ask."

He chuckled, obviously relieved I had made it easier for him to continue.

"I just want you to know that there is always a room for you in my house." He leaned back and took a deep breath as he waited to see how I reacted.

"You want me to move in?"

"What I'm saying is that you are always welcome."

"I don't know what to say. Thank you."

He relaxed his posture and let out a sigh of relief. "Good, I just wanted you to know that."

We drank our tea and didn't say much after that. It felt like a momentous moment had occurred between us and further conversation would have been anti-climactic in a weird sort of way.

Rays of dusty sunlight that shone from between breaks in the clouds moved across the window like beams from a dying torch. Outside, life continued in the form of strangers passing by, each person absorbed with their own thoughts, and perhaps, their own problems.

I pondered on Robert's offer while walking home alone. I desperately wanted to get out of Grandpa's house and away from his insufferable behaviour, but I wasn't sure if I was ready to live with my father, or if I'd ever be.

Peter was home, sitting alone in the parlour and looking like he had nothing of value but his memories of Grandma.

"Were you fighting with Grandpa again?" I asked.

"I can't stand it anymore," he said, his eyes full of despondency and his voice echoing his despair. "I swear I'll kill him if I stay here any longer."

"You don't mean that, do you?"

"Who knows?" He shrugged.

"Why don't you move out?" I asked, knowing what his answer would be.

"And go where? I've no money, Anna. Not a single penny to my name. That bastard was right about one thing. Anything I get, I waste on drink."

I sat down to face him, aware of his pain and feelings of

hopelessness.

"Why don't you stop drinking and save your money? In a few months, you could have the deposit for a flat of your own. Maybe you could even get a job." I tried to sound encouraging, but when I looked into his eyes, I realised my enthusiasm went no farther than my own voice. His expression answered me long before he uttered a reply.

"I can't stop drinking, Anna. Don't think I haven't tried before, because I have, many times. You wouldn't know this, but a few years ago, Mum talked the Jesuits into taking me into a rehab programme they run for people like me."

"No, I didn't know."

He smiled and started to look more cheerful as he remembered back.

"They take you in for a couple of weeks, dry you out, and fill your head with stuff about God loving you, and how you are going to become a better person."

"How did you get on?"

"It was okay while I was there, but after the two weeks, they blessed me and told me 'To go with God.' Well, if God was with me, the first place I brought him was the local bar for a good ole piss up."

"I'm sorry, Peter."

"Don't be sorry for me. I've made my own bed, so now I'll have to lie in it. Think of yourself, Anna. Get out of here and away from him before he fills your head with so much shit that you start believing it."

I left him there, sitting alone in the dim light from the weak ceiling bulb, and went to bed. I tossed and turned for hours before I fell asleep. All the worries that cluttered my mind continued plaguing me in my dreams. When I awoke the next morning, nothing had changed, and nothing had improved.

I ate my breakfast, which consisted of a bowl of porridge and dry toast. While I ate, I felt the intense glare of Grandpa's eyes boring into me from across the kitchen table.

"Where are you going at night?" he growled.

"What do you mean?"

"I mean, why are you coming home late every night? Where do you go after work?"

His abruptness never failed to take me by surprise, and I stuttered, "Just with friends, that's all."

"Why are you lying to me?"

"I'm not lying."

"You have a boyfriend, don't you?"

Again, his question caught me unawares and I was about to say, no, but something stopped me. I didn't know what it was and just assumed it was a sort of courage growing inside me. Later on, I realised it was anger—a slow rage that was born on learning how he had treated my mother. He himself had ensured my ire did not dissipate and fuelled it by his piggishness manner.

I looked up and held his glare. "Yes, I have a boyfriend," I said defiantly.

There was a long silence as my answer sunk into the recesses of his closed mind. His face grew steadily redder and I waited, expected him to explode in an angry rage.

"Who is he?" he said calmly, but his words and tone were laced with venom.

"You don't know him."

"It's that man that was slobbering all over you at the end of the street, isn't it?"

"Pierre?"

"Yes, that's him, the foreign one."

"And what if it is?"

"How old is he?"

"I don't want to have this conversation," I said, standing up. "It's got nothing to do with you." I turned to leave.

"You're no better than your mother. A brazen hussy, that's what you are."

I turned back to face him. "How dare you talk about my mother like that?"

He smiled, seemingly pleased he had gotten a reaction. "She disgraced this family and now it's happening all over again. Like mother like daughter is what I say. I bet your bastard won't know who his father was either."

"You're a bitter and twisted old man, and now you mention it, my father's name is Robert Cleary."

His eyes widened in shock and his reply seemed to get stuck in his throat, leaving him speechless.

"That's right, Grandpa, I know exactly who my father is, and I know how you lied to him, telling him my mother lost the baby and went to England."

He waved me away with his hand, looking at me as if I was nothing better than a piece of dirt. "I want you out of this house. I only agreed to take you in because your grandmother begged me."

"Begged you? Doesn't that tell you something? What wife should have to beg her husband for anything?"

He continued to wave his arm, informing me to go.

I went upstairs and packed my one and only suitcase.

Within the hour, and barely twenty-four hours after Robert offered me a home, he opened his door to find his red-eyed daughter standing on his doorstep.

Thirty-Five

"Anna?" Robert looked at me in surprise, his eyes dropping down to take in my suitcase before looking back up again. His expression was as if his face had frozen in a state of disbelief.

"If this is a bad idea—"

"No, no!" He blurted the words out before I could finish. "I'm sorry. It's just that I never thought you would make your mind up so soon."

"Well, Grandpa helped to speed up my decision."

"Oh, I see." He nodded as if that didn't surprise him. "Come in, come in," he said enthusiastically as he began to regain his senses.

Robert's house had a refreshing feel about it. It was something I hadn't noticed at the dinner party. It was an impression that was exemplified in the daylight. The floors were wooden, a mixture of beech and pine, except for the kitchen, which was tiled. There was no wallpaper. Instead, the walls were smoothly plastered with each room painted in a different bright colour. Modern paintings hung strategically throughout the house and I studied them carefully, trying to decide if they were created by talented artists or if they were expressions reflecting the tormented minds of their creators.

We sat drinking coffee in the kitchen, surrounded by contemporary black cabinets and shiny countertops that had a marble effect.

"I feel like I'm dreaming," he said with glee in his eyes. "I can't believe I'm sitting here with my daughter. After all these years, I mean."

"I won't stay long, just until I find somewhere."

"There's no hurry, Anna. This house is as much yours as it is mine."

"You're very kind, thank you."

"No, I don't just mean there's no hurry in moving."

"I don't understand."

He straightened up in his chair, as if preparing to deliver a rehearsed speech. "I paid a visit to my solicitor a couple days ago. He's in the process of changing the name on the deeds to the house. Legally, it will be in both our names. And should I ever go to the great schoolhouse in the sky, you will own it outright."

"Are you serious?"

"I've never been more serious in my life."

"But you had no idea if I was even going to move in."

"That was irrelevant as far as I was concerned. Even if you never did, or even if you decided to have no further contact with me, it wouldn't have altered my decision."

"I don't know what to say."

"You don't have to say anything."

"But you can't leave me your house."

"Why not? You are my daughter, after all. It's either you or the cat and dogs' home," he said, and then laughed.

"But what about Yvonne?"

"Yvonne is a good friend. We see one another for a weekend every few weeks or so. But you are family to me, Anna. There's a world of difference."

I was stuck for words, overwhelmed by his actions and having no clue as to what to say to him.

"Come on," he said, getting to his feet and lightening the mood with a smile. "Enough of the serious talk. I'll show you your room."

While Robert Cleary seemed to be well organized and had everything sorted out, my bedroom was the one thing he hadn't prepared.

"I was intending to clean it out next weekend," he said with a look of embarrassment.

The room was twice the size of the one in Ignatius Road, but it had become a dumping ground for every item Robert could not bear to throw out over the years. Great stacks of books, their covers coated with dust, stood waist high, and many leaned precariously like the Tower of Pisa. I could see the brass leg of a bed, but that was all as the rest of it was buried under a heap of cardboard boxes, every one of them overflowing with junk of one kind or another.

For the rest of the afternoon, we worked at clearing out the room. It didn't seem like work as such. We had fun going through the contents of each box. Every item was checked by Robert before deciding which pile it would go to. Had I not been there to coax him, everything would have simply been shoved up into the attic. But with some gentle persuasion, most of what came out of the room would be destined to go to one of the local charity shops. Only those items Robert would rather die than part with found themselves in the attic pile.

When we finally finished, I had my own bedroom, which consisted of a brass bed, built-in storage cupboards, and a large mahogany chest of drawers. The window was east facing and the evening sun warmed the room and shined off the varnished floorboards. I emptied my suitcase onto the bed and began to put my clothes away. My lack of belongings quickly became glaringly obvious with all the free storage space left over.

Robert cooked dinner and for the rest of the evening, fussed over me like a mother hen. When darkness came, we drew the curtains, lit the fire, and talked while drinking wine.

"Have you made up your mind about London yet?"

"No, not yet."

"It's a great opportunity for you."

"I know it is, and I'm very grateful. Please don't think my not making a decision yet is because I don't realise that."

"What's keeping you from making that decision?"

"Pierre has asked me to return to France with him."

"Oh, I see..." His look of disappointment was evident despite his attempts to hide it.

There was a moment of silence. I knew he was dying to say something, to tell me it would be a foolish move to turn my back on college. But he held his opinion behind pursed lips, still believing he had no right to interfere in my affairs.

"What do you think I should do?" I asked, feeling as if I

was throwing a drowning man a lifeline.

"Well, if you what my honest opinion..." He sat upright, grateful for the opening I had given him.

"I do. Please tell me what you really think."

"I can see the appeal of going to France. Pierre seems like a decent guy and from his description of Bordeaux, it does sound ideal."

"But..." I coaxed him to continue.

"But you have your whole life ahead of you. Be practical, Anna, you have no money and no qualifications to speak of. What if things don't work out? What will you do then?"

I didn't answer.

"I'm sorry, Anna. I know it's not what you want to hear, but I can't lie to you. What I'm saying I would say to any of my students. It's not just because you are my daughter."

"I know. Deep down, I know you are right."

"Just think about it, that's all. Whatever you decide, I'll help in whatever way I can."

The conversation ended there. I had known what his view would be before I asked him. I think I just needed to hear it said out loud.

Thirty-Six

The infernal racket continued to sound. It invaded my
dreams like an unwanted bee buzzing in my ear. I told it to
go away, calmly at first, but then with increased irritation as
I yelled at the annoying pest. I rolled over and tried to block
out the sound by pulling the blankets up and around my
head, but still the noise tormented me without abate. My
eyelids struggled to open, the dawn light assaulting my
senses in a burning tide of luminous energy. As my eyes ad-
justed to the early morning brightness, the infuriating bee
returned to pester me. It was only then I realised it was the
doorbell that had woken me. It continued to sound as if
someone had their finger pressed hard against it.

I stumbled down the stairs, swaying like a drunkard, trying to fix my dressing gown and rub my tired eyes at the
same time.

"All right, all right," I muttered as I fumbled with the door
latch. "Pierre?"

"I'm sorry, I know it's early. Can I come in?"

He followed me into the kitchen and I started to fill the
kettle as he sat down. He looked troubled and it worried me.

"What's wrong, Pierre?"

Before he could answer, Robert walked in, his eyes
squinting as if in pain from the dusty rays of sunlight stream-
ing in the window.

"Pierre?" he said with the same questionable voice I had
used at the door.

"I'm sorry, Mr Cleary."

"Robert, call me, Robert."

Pierre nodded.

"Is everything okay?" Robert asked, looking from me to Pierre, unsure who would answer his question.

"No, it's not," Pierre said, and then turned to me. "Please sit down, Anna. I need to tell you something."

I stopped what I was doing. The ominous tone in his voice startled me.

Robert appeared to feel awkward and was about to leave us alone, but Pierre stopped him.

"Mr Cleary, I think you had better stay."

Robert sat down, not bothering to remind Pierre to call him by his Christian name.

"The reason I've called so early is because there might be news about Rebecca."

"Might be?" Robert asked.

"Yes. I don't know anything for certain yet."

"What's happened?" I asked, my voice breaking in fear of his response.

"I was woken at four a.m. this morning by the hotel receptionist. She told me there were two detectives in the lobby, and they wanted to talk to me. I went down to them. They said they called to your grandfather's house, but he couldn't tell them where you had gone."

"How did they know to contact you at the hotel?" Robert asked.

"I gave my details when we reported her missing."

"What did they say? Is she in trouble?" I asked, or rather, pleaded for an answer.

Pierre focused his look on me. I'd never seen such a solemn expression on a man's face before.

"They found a body in the canal."

"Oh my God," I gasped. In a mere instant, every ounce of strength seemed to be sucked from my body as an overwhelming wave of weakness enveloped me. I felt like throwing up.

"Was it Rebecca?" Robert calmly asked, although his voice sounded different, as if he was fighting some obstruction in his throat.

"They don't know. They want us to go to the City Morgue and see if we can identify the body."

"No," Robert said sternly. "There is no way Anna can do

that. We'll go with you, but it would be better if you went in alone, don't you agree?"

He was asking Pierre, but I nodded in agreement, although I did not really understand the question. My whole thought process had ground to a standstill as if my brain was clogged with some sort of sticky glue.

Robert stood up. "We'll get dressed and then I'll get the car ready."

I didn't remember getting ready. It must have been one of those actions carried out by some sort of autopilot device in my brain, some emergency resource that engaged when I ceased to function properly. I didn't even recall getting into the car. A vague recollection of their voices as we drove through the empty streets was all I did remember. What they said, I couldn't say. Their voices sounded distant, as if part of some confused dream.

We pulled into the City Morgue's entrance, our path blocked by tall wooden gates that had long strips of blue paint peeling off around the edges.

Robert got out and pressed a button fixed to the pillar.

A few moments later, one of the gates opened inwards, just enough for a man to stick his head out. They exchanged words and the man nodded in a way that gave the impression we were expected.

The gates opened and we drove in. We were directed into an office where we sat facing an official who seemed neither friendly nor sympathetic. He was a thin man with a pointy chin and small, penetrating eyes that held no expression in them. It transpired that he was expecting us, having been informed by the detective that visited Pierre. He filled out several official-looking forms, for which he asked us questions about Rebecca and about our own identities.

I sat quietly, too numb to talk. I nodded whenever he asked me something, and either Pierre or Robert gave my answer for me. When the paperwork was complete, he led us out of the office and along corridors that reeked of disinfectant. I felt ill just being there, and an urge to run from the building and out into the fresh air almost overcame me.

We went into a small waiting room, the bareness of which was only eased by three plastic chairs and a small wooden table, its surface barely a foot of the blandly tiled floor. There were a handful of magazines on the table, the sort that would be found in any doctor's office. *Who would want or even be able to read something at a time like this*? I thought.

"Now," the man said, making sure he had our attention. "Who is going to view the body?"

The word *body* sent a sickening surge of bile swirling around my stomach. He uttered it so clinically and with such coldness I wanted to shout at him, *That's a girl in there, and not a body!*

"I will go in," Pierre said, stepping forward.

I moved, too, although I said nothing, but Robert took hold of my hand. When I looked around, he was shaking his head slowly, his eyes silently begging me to stay where I was.

We waited while Pierre went into the viewing room to observe a corpse. Was it Rebecca? The question screamed continuously inside my head, so loud that the silent words seemed to echo off the bare walls of the room. I convinced myself against all reasoning that the unfortunate girl would not be my friend. The thought of it being so was too unimaginable to seem possible.

Yet when Pierre returned, the absolute shock in his eyes confirmed my worst nightmare. He stepped closer to hold me just as my legs lost all their strength, leaving me limp and lifeless like a ragdoll in his embrace. While my body seemed to lose all power, I was aware of being guided back into a chair by both Pierre and Robert. I could hear their voices reassuring me, but their words seemed garbled, as if they were speaking underwater. If I could have described myself at that moment, I resembled a traumatised survivor pulled from a collapsed building—too shocked and too dazed to be aware of anything but my own confusion.

I waited with Robert in the car while Pierre stayed inside to fill out more forms. When he came out, he mentioned something about an inquest that would have to be held. I wasn't listening to him. I just wanted to get home. I wanted to lock myself in my room and shut out the world with all its pain and cruelty.

Thirty-Seven

Once again, life changed for me. Each traumatic event hit me like a sledge hammer trying to smash a boulder, each blow forever altering the stone's shape. First my mother, then Grandma, and now my friend. I wondered if there would be any end to the heartbreak that seemed to walk alongside me through life. It was as if anyone that made me happy paid for it with their own life. Who would be next? Pierre? Maybe even Robert, who was trying so hard to make me happy. What would his reward be? I tried to dispel all the depressing thoughts from my head. I imagined what Grandma or Mother would have said to me on hearing such negative views. Thinking of their advice, which always seemed strengthened through bitter experience, I felt as if there was no alternative but to stand up and solider on.

An inquest into Rebecca's death was held two days later. Pierre attended, but insisted I did not go. When I found out that the entire procedure lasted no more than fifteen minutes, it saddened me. It seemed nothing more than an opportunity for faceless officials to stamp their forms and file them away to be forgotten.

"The sergeant from the Garda station was there," Pierre said.

"The one we made our report to?"

"Yes. He explained the situation to the coroner, who seemed content that further enquiries were not necessary."

"So that's it."

"Yes, Anna, it's over now."

"Over?"

"Yes, it's over."

"You don't really think that, do you, Pierre?"

"I don't understand, Anna, what are you saying?"

"Why did she kill herself?"

"Because she was depressed."

"And that's it, she was depressed?"

"Yes, what are you trying to say?"

"Don't you think we share the blame?"

"The blame for what?"

"For what happened to her."

"Anna." He reached out to grasp my hand. "It was her decision, hers alone. You should not feel guilt for her actions."

"You don't see it, do you?"

He looked at me with a confused expression. I knew at that moment he would never understand.

"I know it was her decision, but don't you think we played a part in sending her to the canal that night?"

"No, I don't. I think you are wrong in trying to shoulder some of the blame. Even if she was wronged by others, she made her own choices in life."

"And death."

"Yes, I suppose. Anyway, it's finished now. We have to think about our own future."

"Do we have one?"

"Anna, you can still come to France with me. When you see the vineyard, you will forget all about this, I promise."

I didn't answer. Robert came in and the subject changed. I studied Pierre's face as he chatted with him. He had already forgotten. I could see that. I could read it in his eyes and see it in his smile.

Rebecca was buried seven days after her body was pulled from the dark waters of the canal. All the arrangements were made by the Sisters of Charity. The nuns that had reared her, and whom Rebecca had so often criticized, took her back into their fold to send her on her last journey.

There weren't many at the funeral. I stood over the graveside, riddled with guilt and regret. Rodrigo and Petra came with some others from the hotel. It was the first time I remembered seeing Rodrigo without a smile upon his face. At some point, I cried in his arms and felt his body tremble with heartbreak.

"I did this to her, Rodrigo," I said through quivering lips.

He pushed me back a little, a look on his face that was somewhere between surprise and anger. For a moment, I thought he was going to yell at me.

"My little one, don't ever say or think such things as this. It hurt me to say, but no one is responsible. Only Rebecca."

"You don't understand," I said, trying to compose myself. "I betrayed her."

"You talk nonsense, I think. I know you think you take this Frenchman from Rebecca and because you do this thing, you feel responsible?"

I nodded.

"Anna, you must put these silly thoughts out from you mind. Is it not true that Frenchman and Rebecca were no more when you go meet him?"

"Yes," I said. "But she still wanted to be with him."

"Oh, Anna, you silly child. If I miss the sunset and do harm to myself, is it the fault of the night?"

"No, of course not, but it's not exactly the same thing, is it, Rodrigo?"

"No, it's not, but the ridiculousness of the idea is the same. You think you hold some blame for this terrible thing, but you are no more to blame than the night is for swallowing the sun."

I left Rodrigo, feeling slightly better. There was something unique about the man from the Basque country that I'd never known anyone else to possess. His jovial nature, his honesty, which seemed to make him incapable of lying, was like a sedative to my troubled mind. Just hearing his voice was enough to cheer me up, regardless of what he might be talking about.

"Maybe we should go now?" Robert asked.

I shrugged, knowing we had to leave at some time but feeling reluctant to walk away, as if it was closing some sort of door between us and Rebecca.

"Yes, maybe we should," Pierre said.

Feeling outvoted and unable to present any logical reason that I could put into words, we left the graveyard. The sad serenity of the cemetery was slowly replaced by the noise of traffic as we emerged back into the streets of Dublin's inner city.

Thirty-Eight

A cold breeze whipped around my ankles. The park was devoid of people bar the hardened dog walkers who came out regardless of the weather. It seemed right to meet Pierre here. Stephen's Green was where Rebecca and I would go on warm days during our lunch break. It wasn't the same any-more and I knew it would never be again. Whenever I would sit on one of its benches, the empty seat beside me would echo the void in my heart.

The water's dark surface was a reflection of the dull sky above. I was glad the sun was not shining. It wasn't a morn-ing to feel or deserve the pleasant heat of the sun.

"Anna?" Pierre's voice came from behind, and I turned to see his face of apprehension. I wondered if he had guessed my reason for summoning him. "I got your note," he said.

"Thanks for coming."

"It's nice here," he said, sitting down and looking out across the lake.

"This is where we would sometimes come at lunch hour," I said.

"We?"

"Rebecca and I."

"Oh, I see."

He went quiet for a while. I knew he did not want to hear her name, but I wanted to say it. I wanted to hear it said out loud even if it was only my own words I was hearing.

"I've accepted a college placement in London."

"The place Robert organised?"

"Yes."

"And what about us?" he asked.

"Us?"

"Yes. Us going to France."

"I thought it was a good idea for a while, but now..." My words trailed off as if they were being dissolved into the cold air.

"I don't understand. What changed your mind?"

"There can be no future for us, Pierre. We would never find peace together."

"Anna, you have to forget about Rebecca."

"I don't want to forget. And even if I did, how could I? There would always be three of us, Pierre. She would always be there, reminding us of what we did."

"I have told you before, you are wrong to blame yourself."

"I'm not blaming myself. I know I'm not responsible for her death. But she was my friend and I don't want to forget her. And I know, if we are together, I'll never be able to mention her name. It would be like a wedge keeping us apart. It would always be there, no matter how much you deny its existence."

He sighed deeply before speaking. "So, this is the end for us?"

"The end for us was when she threw herself into the water. She didn't just end her own life that night. She ended any future we might have had together."

I hadn't noticed his hand on mine until that point. The feeling of his fingers slipping away made me aware that his hand had been over mine.

"I don't agree with you, Anna, but I can see now that I'll never make you see differently."

"I'm sorry, Pierre."

"You've nothing to be sorry for, Anna." He smiled and it was a smile that held both sorrow and good wishes for me.

I stayed while he got up and walked out of my life. His footsteps faded into the distance while I watched a gull sweep down from the sky and dive into the lake. It was a good ten seconds before the bird broke the water's surface and struggled to gain height. There was a small fish in its mouth and droplets of water were thrown out from its flapping wings.

I thought Robert was going to cry. I stood outside the

ferry terminal with two suitcases beside me.

"Well, this is it," he said.

"Yes, I suppose so," I replied with embarrassment for not knowing what to say to him. He had a look of pride in his eyes. It was the look only a parent could know. "I want to thank you, Robert, for all you have done for me."

"There's no need to thank me. You are my daughter, after all."

"And you are my father," I said with a smile.

He stepped forward and hugged me.

"Don't wait," I said when he released me. "I don't think I could bear waving from the boat."

"I understand. Don't forget you are coming back during the summer break," he said, looking as if he was unsure what my reply would be.

"I won't, but I don't want to come back and find my room cluttered with junk."

"Scout's honour," he said, holding up two fingers before he laughed.

I watched his car drive out of the carpark. There was happiness in my heart knowing I would see him again during the holidays.

I stood at the rear rail of the Dublin to Holyhead ferry. It was six a.m. and dirty grey clouds rolled across the city to create a truly depressing image of dawn. I watched the foaming wake of water leave a wide trail as the ferry left the harbour. The two tall towers of the Ringsend power station stood defiantly, and plumes of dense smoke billowed out to mix with the darkening clouds above.

There was a low and continuous drone from the ship's engines, interrupted only by the squawks of terns as they hovered close to the water's surface. I envied their indifference to the cold as they plunged headfirst into the murky depths in search of small fish.

The sky continued to darken and rain began to fall. I retreated inside and found an empty seat. I looked around at my fellow passengers. I could not see a single cheerful face. I doubted if I looked cheerful either. They, like I, had probably stirred from a warm bed in the middle of the night to make the early crossing. The day had barely begun and we were already exhausted.

Napping during the journey was impossible. As we left Dublin Port, the choppiness of the open sea increased until I felt as if I was on a fairground ride. It was not long before the foul smell of vomit filled the cabin air. There was a steady stream of green-faced passengers making their way to and from the toilets. My own stomach turned over with queasiness. I think I would have been all right had I not had to watch others practically racing toward the toilets. Some did not make it that far. The floor became awash with puke as it flowed from one side to the other with each roll of the ship. I decided to go out onto the deck, despite the drizzling rain. I sat on a bench and watched the relentless grey swell for the remainder of the four hour journey.

It was a relief to walk onto dry land when we reached Holyhead.

Fifteen minutes later, I was sitting on the train watching the last passengers get aboard. We had barely left the train station when I fell asleep. The rhythmic *clickety-clack* lulled me with its soothing melody, like a baby being rocked in their cot.

The moment I stepped off the train, I was confronted with a scene of mass organised bedlam, if indeed there was such a thing. Hundreds, maybe thousands of people filled Victoria Station. They crisscrossed one another as they all hurried in their intended directions. No one seemed to acknowledge anyone else, except what might have been necessary to ensure they did not collide. The station was huge, much bigger than train or bus stations in Ireland. The vast building was well-lit with shafts of hazy daylight coming through hundreds of Perspex panels in the roof.

The noise was what struck me most, even more than the busyness of the place. Klaxon speakers were everywhere, bolted to iron roof beams. A voice droned almost constantly through the speakers, announcing both bus and train schedules. The words from the speakers were barely decipherable, and I wondered if it was just me that struggled to understand the voice.

I emerged from the station into the busy street and wondered what would become of my decision to go to London.

About the Author

Stephen O'Sullivan lives in Dublin City, Ireland. He works as a service technician for an international security company.

He first put pen to paper several years ago when his young daughter asked him to write a story for her. After just a few sentences, he was addicted to writing and hasn't paused since.

Anna is Stephen's second book. His debut novel, Andersons's Gold, was published in 2013 by *Whimsical Publications*.

As well as writing novels, Stephen has a particular passion for writing short stories. His tales have appeared in many well-known magazines and his work has been featured in the *Irish Times* Newspaper.

.

www.ingramcontent.com/pod-product-compliance
Lightning Source LLC
Chambersburg PA
CBHW030755210626
46807CB00017B/2525